Also by Julian Barnes

FICTION

Metroland
Before She Met Me
Flaubert's Parrot
Staring at the Sun
A History of the World in 10 ½ Chapters
Talking It Over
The Porcupine
Cross Channel
England, England
Love, etc.
The Lemon Table
Arthur & George
Pulse
The Sense of an Ending
The Noise of Time
The Only Story

NONFICTION

Letters from London 1990–1995
Something to Declare
The Pedant in the Kitchen
Nothing to Be Frightened Of
Through the Window
Levels of Life
Keeping an Eye Open
The Man in the Red Coat

TRANSLATION

In the Land of Pain
by Alphonse Daudet

ELIZABETH FINCH

ELIZABETH FINCH

A NOVEL

JULIAN BARNES

Alfred A. Knopf
New York
2022

Library of Congress Cataloging-in-Publication Data
Names: Barnes, Julian, author.
Title: Elizabeth Finch : a novel / Julian Barnes.
Description: First United States edition. | New York : Alfred A. Knopf, 2022.
Identifiers: LCCN 2022004061 (print) | LCCN 2022004062 (ebook) |
ISBN 9780593535431 (hardcover) | ISBN 9780593535448 (ebook)
Subjects: LCGFT: Novels.
Classification: LCC PR6052.A6657 E45 2022 (print) | LCC PR6052.A6657
(ebook) | DDC 823/.914—dc23/eng/20220127
LC record available at https://lccn.loc.gov/2022004061
LC ebook record available at https://lccn.loc.gov/2022004062

Jacket photograph by MirageC / Moment / Getty Images
Jacket design by Janet Hansen

Manufactured in the United States of America
First United States Edition

to Rachel

ONE

She stood before us, without notes, books or nerves. The lectern was occupied by her handbag. She looked around, smiled, was still, and began.

"You will have observed that the title of this course is 'Culture and Civilisation.' Do not be alarmed. I shall not be pelting you with pie charts. I shall not attempt to stuff you with facts as a goose is stuffed with corn; this would only lead to an engorged liver, which would be unhealthy. Next week I shall supply you with a reading list which is entirely optional; you will neither lose marks for ignoring it, nor gain them by relentless study. I shall teach you as the adults you undoubtedly are. The best form of education, as the Greeks knew, is collaborative. But I am no Socrates and you are not a classroom of Platos, if that is the correct plural form. Nonetheless, we shall engage in dialogue. At the same time—and since you are no longer in primary school—I shall not dispense milksop encouragement and bland approval. For some of you, I may well not be the best teacher, in the sense of the one most suited to your temperament and cast of mind. I mention this in advance to those for whom it will be the case. Naturally, I hope you will find the course interesting, and, indeed, fun. Rigorous fun, that is. The terms are not incompatible. And I shall expect rigour from you in return. Winging it will not suit. My name is Elizabeth Finch. Thank you."

And she smiled again.

None of us had taken a note. We gazed back at her, some

in awe, a few in puzzlement bordering on irritation, others already half in love.

I can't remember what she taught us in that first lesson. But I knew obscurely that, for once in my life, I had arrived at the right place.

Her clothes. Let's start at ground level. She wore brogues, black in winter, brown suede in autumn and spring. Stockings or tights—you never saw Elizabeth Finch with bare legs (and you certainly couldn't imagine her in beachwear). Skirts just below the knee—she resisted the annual hemline tyranny. Indeed, she appeared to have settled on her look some time ago. It could still be called stylish; another decade, and it might be antique or, perhaps, vintage. In summer, a box-pleated skirt, usually navy; tweed in winter. Sometimes she adopted a tartan or kiltish look with a big silver safety pin (no doubt there's a special Scottish word for it). Obvious money was spent on blouses, in silk or fine cotton, often striped, and in no way translucent. Occasionally a brooch, always small and, as they say, discreet, yet somehow refulgent. She rarely wore earrings (were her lobes even pierced? now there's a question). On her left little finger, a silver ring which we took to be inherited, rather than bought or given. Her hair was a kind of sandy grey, shapely and of unvarying length. I imagined a regular fortnightly appointment. Well, she believed in artifice, as she told us more than once. And artifice, as she also observed, was not incompatible with truth.

Though we—her students—were between our late twenties and early forties, we at first responded to her like kids back at school. We wondered about her background and her private life, about why and whether she had never—as far as we knew—married. About what she did in the evenings. Did she make herself a perfect *fines herbes* omelette, have a single glass of wine (Elizabeth Finch drunk? only if the world turned upside down) while reading the latest fascicle of *Goethe Studies*? You see how easy it was to stray into fantasy, even satire.

·

She smoked all the years I knew her. And again, she didn't smoke like anyone else. There are smokers who patently enjoy every burst of nicotine; others who inhale with a sense of self-loathing; some display it as a style habit; others again, annoyingly, claim to have "only one or two a day," as if they were in charge of their addiction. And—since all smokers lie—"one or two" always turns out to mean three or four, even half a pack. EF, on the other hand, displayed no attitude to her smoking. It was something she did which required neither explanation nor ornamentation. She decanted her cigarettes into a tortoiseshell case, which left us playing Guess the Brand. She smoked as if she were indifferent to smoking. Does that make sense? And if you had dared to ask her, she wouldn't have fallen back on excuses. Yes, she would have said, of course she was addicted; and yes, she knew it was bad for her, and also antisocial. But no, she wasn't going to stop, or count how many she smoked a day; such matters were very low on her list of concerns. And since—this was my own personal deduction, or rather, guess—since she had no fear of death and nowadays judged life somewhat overrated, the question was really of no interest to her, and therefore shouldn't be to you either.

Naturally, she suffered migraines.

★

In my mind's eye—my memory's eye, the only place I can see her—she is standing before us, preternaturally still. She had none of those lecturer's tics and tricks designed to charm, distract, or indicate character. She never waved her arms about or supported her chin in her hand. She might occasionally put a slide up to illustrate a point, but that was mostly unnecessary. She commanded attention by her stillness and her voice. It was a calm, clear voice enriched by decades of smoking. She wasn't one of those teachers who only engaged with their students when they looked up from their notes because, as I said, she didn't lecture from notes. It was all in her head fully thought out, fully processed. This also compelled attention, reducing the gap between her and us.

Her diction was formal, her sentence structure entirely grammatical—indeed, you could almost hear the commas, semicolons and full stops. She never started a sentence without knowing how and when it would end. Yet she never sounded like a talking book. Her vocabulary was drawn from the same word-box she used for both writing and general conversation. And yet the effect wasn't archaic in any way, it was intensely alive. And she enjoyed—perhaps to amuse herself, or to surprise us—throwing in the occasional phrase of a different tonality.

For instance, one week she was talking to us about *The Golden Legend*, that medieval assemblage of miracles and martyrdoms. Gaudy miracles and instructive martyrdoms. Her subject was St. Ursula.

"Cast your minds back, if you will, to AD 400, a time before Christian hegemony had been established on our shores. Ursula was a British princess, daughter of the Christian King Nothus. She was wise, dutiful, devout and virtuous—all the usual moral accoutrements of such princesses. Also beautiful, that more problematic accoutrement. Prince Etherius, son of the King of Anglia, fell in love with her and asked for her hand in marriage. This placed Ursula's father in a dilemma, since the Angles were not only very powerful, but also worshippers of idols.

"Ursula was a bride to be bartered, like many before and since; and being wise, virtuous, et cetera, she was also ingenious. Accept the offer from the son of Power, she told her father; yet attach conditions which will impose delay. Ask to be granted three years of grace, so that Ursula could make a pilgrimage to Rome, during which time young Etherius was to be instructed in the true faith and then baptised. Some might judge this a deal-breaker, but not the love-struck Etherius. The views of the King of Anglia are not recorded.

"When news of Ursula's planned spiritual escapade got out, other like-minded virgins flocked to her side. And here we hit upon a textual nub. As many of you will know, Ursula was accompanied by eleven thousand virgins; those of you familiar with Venice might recall Carpaccio's sequential representation of the story. Such a package tour to organise, and Mr. Thomas Cook had yet to be born. The textual nub I mentioned concerns the letter M, and what the original scribe meant by it. Was it M for *Mille*, thousand, or M for *Martyr*? Some of us might find the latter reading more plausible. Ursula plus eleven virgin martyrs makes twelve, also the number of Christ's Apostles.

"Still, let us allow the story to proceed in Technicolor and CinemaScope, techniques which Carpaccio did much to popularise. Eleven thousand virgins set off from Britain. When they reached Cologne, an angel of the Lord appeared to Ursula, with the message that after leaving Rome she and her cortège were to return via Cologne, where they were to acquire the holy crown of martyrdom. News of this endgame spread through the eleven thousand, to be greeted with staunch rapture. Meanwhile, in Britain, another of the Lord's ubiquitous angels appeared to Etherius, instructing him to meet his intended bride in Cologne, where he would also acquire the palm of martyrdom.

"Everywhere she went, Ursula attracted more and more followers, though the total is not recorded. In Rome, the very Pope joined this female host, and in doing so brought upon himself calumny and excommunication. Meanwhile again, two villainous Roman commanders, fearing that the hysterical success of the expedition would further the spread of Christianity, arranged for a Hunnish army to massacre the returning pilgrims. Conveniently, a Hunnish army happened to be besieging Cologne at that very time. We must allow for such narrative coincidences and angelic interventions: this is not, after all, a nineteenth-century novel. Although, as I say that, nineteenth-century novels are full of coincidence.

"And so Ursula and her vast entourage reached Cologne, whereupon the Hunnish army turned away from their siege machinery and began slaughtering the Eleven Thousand Plus with—and the phrase was a banality even in AD 400—'the savagery of wolves falling upon a flock of sheep.'"

Elizabeth Finch paused, surveyed the room and asked, "What are we to make of all this?" And into the silence she gave her reply: "I propose: Suicide by Cop."

Elizabeth Finch was not in any way a public figure. You will google her with little result. If asked to characterise her professionally, I would say that she was an independent scholar. That may sound like a euphemism, even a truism. But before knowledge became officially housed in academe, there used to be men and women of the highest intelligence who privately pursued their own interests. Mostly, of course, they had money; some were eccentric, a few certifiably mad. But money allowed them to travel and research what and where they needed, with no pressure to publish, colleagues to outperform or heads of department to satisfy.

I never knew Elizabeth Finch's financial position. I imagined she had family money, or an inheritance. She had a West London flat in which I never set foot; she appeared to live frugally; I assume she arranged her teaching to allow her time for private, independent scholarship. She had published two books: *Explosive Women*, about female anarchists in London between 1890 and 1910; and *Our Necessary Myths*, about nationalism, religion and family. Both were short, and both out of print. To some an independent scholar whose books are unavailable might seem a laughable figure. As opposed to the scores of tenured dolts and bores who would have done better to keep silent.

Several of her students subsequently made their names. She is acknowledged in some books of medieval history and female thought. But she was not known to those who did not know her. Which may sound self-evident. Except that nowadays, in the digital landscape, friends and followers have come to mean different, watered-down things. Many people know one another without knowing them at all. And are happy with that superficiality.

You might think me old-fashioned (but my case is not relevant). You might think Elizabeth Finch equally, if not more, old-fashioned. But if she was, it was not in the normal way, that of embodying a previous generation whose truths had now proved wan and withered. How can I put it? She dealt in truths not from previous generations but from previous eras, truths she kept alive but which others had abandoned. And I don't mean anything like "she was an old-fashioned Tory/liberal/socialist." She was outside of her age in many ways. "Do not be taken in by time," she once said, "and imagine that history—and especially intellectual history—is linear." She was high-minded, self-sufficient, European. And as I write those words, I stop, because I hear in my head something she once taught us in class: "And remember, whenever you see a character in a novel, let alone a biography or history book, reduced and neatened into three adjectives, always distrust that description." It is a rule of thumb I have tried to obey.

The class soon shook down into groups and cliques, by the usual method of hazard and intent. Some of it was based on the choice of drink after class: beer, wine, beer and/or wine and/or anything else in a bottle, fruit juice, nothing at all. My group, which shifted easily between beer and wine, consisted of Neil (i.e., me), Anna (Dutch, so occasionally outraged by English frivolity), Geoff (provocateur), Linda (emotionally labile, whether it came to study or life itself) and Stevie (town planner looking for more). One of our bonds was, paradoxically, that we rarely agreed about anything, except that whatever government was in power was useless, God almost certainly did not exist, life was for the living, and you could never have too many bar snacks in noisy packets. This was a time before laptops in class and social media out of it; when news came from newspapers and knowledge came from books. Was it a simpler time, or a duller one? Both or neither?

★

"Monotheism," said Elizabeth Finch. "Monomania. Monogamy. Monotony. Nothing good begins this way." She paused. "Monogram—a sign of vanity. Monocle ditto. Monoculture— a precursor to the death of rural Europe. I am prepared to acknowledge the usefulness of a monorail. There are many neutral scientific terms which I am also prepared to admit. But where the prefix applies to human business ... Monoglot, the sign of an enclosed and self-deluding country. The monokini, as facetious an etymology as it is a garment. Monopoly—and I do not refer to the board game—always a disaster if you give it time. Monorchid: a condition to be pitied but not aspired to. Any questions?"

Linda, who often seemed to be suffering from what she quaintly called "heart trouble," asked anxiously, "What have you got against monogamy? Isn't it how most people want to live? Isn't it what most people dream of?"

"Beware of dreams," Elizabeth Finch replied. "Also, as a general rule, beware of what most people aspire to." She paused, half-smiled at Linda and addressed the class through her. "Enforced monogamy is as much to say enforced happiness, which we know is not possible. Unenforced monogamy might seem possible. Romantic monogamy might seem to be desirable. But the first normally collapses back into a version of enforced monogamy, while the second is liable to become obsessive and hysterical. And thereby lies close to monomania. We should always distinguish between mutual passion and shared monomania."

We were all silenced, taking this in. Most of us had had the average sexual and amatory experience of our generation: that's to say, far too much in the opinion of the preceding generation, and pathetically little in the view of the next, pressing generation. We were also wondering how much of what she said was based on personal experience, but none of us dared ask.

Linda, to her credit, pursued the matter. "So are you saying it's all hopeless?"

"How does the witty Mr. Sondheim put it?" And Elizabeth Finch actually half-sang: "'One's impossible, two is dreary, / Three is company, safe and cheery.' Which is one way of looking at the matter, to be sure."

"But do you agree with that, or are you just avoiding the question?"

"No, I am merely offering you the alternatives."

"So are you saying that Etherius was wrong to go to Cologne?" Linda, as we were learning, took classes very personally, even those on medieval religion.

"No, not wrong. We all pursue what we think is best for us, even if it means our extinction. Sometimes, especially if it means that. By the time we attain it, or don't, it is usually too late anyway."

"*That's* not much help," said Linda, with a kind of whiney fierceness.

"I am not employed to help you," replied Elizabeth Finch, firmly and yet not rebukingly. "I am here to assist you to think and argue and develop minds of your own." She paused. "But since you ask about Etherius, let us consider his case. As Ursula's betrothed, he accepted her conditions: that while she undertook her pilgrimage to Rome, he would study the Christian texts, be convinced of their truths, and be baptised into her religion. How much this must have enraged his father, the King of Anglia and a most notorious pagan, we are not told. But in any case, an angel of the Lord appeared to Etherius, instructing him to meet Ursula in Cologne, where they would suffer glorious martyrdom together.

"What are we to make of this? On the emotional level, we might regard it as an extreme, indeed fanatical example of romantic love. In other hands, it might have a Wagnerian aspect to it. On the theological level, his behaviour might be regarded as a gross form of queue-jumping. Also, we must consider the effect of enforced chastity on the young human male—and, for that matter, on the young human female. It can manifest itself in all forms of morbid behaviour. Were Ursula and Etherius, betrothed now for three years, allowed a nuptial night in advance of bending their necks before Teutonic swords and offering their breasts to lances and arrows? We must rather doubt this, for indeed, the conjugal thrill might have changed their minds."

Afterwards, at the student bar, some of us started straight in on the hard stuff.

I trained as an actor; that's how I met my first wife, Joanna. We both had the same inchoate yet unshakeable optimism, at least for the first few years. I got small parts in telly and did voice-overs; together, we wrote scripts and sent them off into the howling winds. Our repertoire also included doing two-hander gigs on cruise ships: comedy, patter, a bit of song and dance. My most consistent source of income was playing a mildly sinister barman in a long-running soap (no, not a famous one). Every so often, for years afterwards, people would accost me with, "You know, you look just like Freddy the Barman in, what was it called—*NW 12* ?" I never correct them to *SE 15*, just smile and demur: "Strange, isn't it, quite a few people have told me that."

I worked in restaurants when the jobs dried up. That's to say, I was a waiter. But I had, or could assume, a presence, so got promoted to front of house. And gradually I stopped resting and then stopped being an actor. I knew some food suppliers, Joanna and I decided to live in the country. I grew mushrooms and, later, hydroponic tomatoes. Our daughter Hannah no longer said, with childish pride, "My dad's on the telly," and bravely tried putting the same verve into "My dad grows mushrooms." Joanna, who was more successful than me at acting, decided it would be better for her career if she lived in London. And if I didn't. So that was that, really. Yes, you can still spot her on telly, she's often in . . . oh, sod it.

When I told Elizabeth Finch that I had been an actor, she smiled. "Ah, acting," she said, "the perfect example of artificiality producing authenticity." It made me feel rather pleased, indeed valued.

EF, as we now privately referred to her, stood before us, handbag on the lectern as usual, and said: "Be approximately satisfied with approximate happiness. The only thing in life which is clear and beyond doubt is unhappiness." And then she waited. We were on our own. Who would dare to speak first?

You will note that the quotation was unattributed. This was deliberate on her part, a useful trick to help us think for ourselves. If she had identified the source, we would start thinking about what we knew of the life and work of the person quoted, and about received opinion. We would bow in reverence accordingly, or the opposite.

And so we had a lively discussion, pitching still-youthful hopefulness against mature scepticism—at least, as we saw it—until she chose to reveal her source.

"Goethe, than whom few of us can hope to live a fuller or more interesting life, stated on his deathbed—he was eighty-two at the time—that he had only ever felt happiness in his life for one quarter of an hour." She didn't raise a physical eyebrow at us—it was not one of her gestures—but she raised a metaphorical, or even moral one. And so, as a class, we took that on board and started discussing whether to be a great—or even minor—intellectual was to be doomed to unhappiness, and whether people on their deathbeds made such remarks (which sounded patently untrue to us) either because they couldn't remember, or because downplaying such a major aspect of their lives made them less reluctant to die. At which point Linda, who was always fearless about saying things the rest of us found naive, if not embarrassing, suggested:

"Perhaps Goethe never found the right woman."

In the presence of another lecturer, we might have felt free to snigger. But EF, while rigorous in her own thought, was never dismissive of our ideas and offerings, however meagre, or sentimental, or hopelessly autobiographical. Instead, she would transform our paltry thoughtlets into something of fuller interest.

"We must certainly consider, not just in this class, but outside it, in our own turbulent and fretful lives, the element of chance. The number of people we deeply meet is strangely few. Passion may mislead us furiously. Reason may mislead us just as much. Our genetic inheritance might hamstring us. So might previous events in our lives. It is not just soldiers in the field who later suffer from post-traumatic stress disorder. It is often the inevitable consequence of a seemingly normal sublunary existence."

At which Linda could not help looking a little content with herself.

★

Obviously, I can't promise that those were exactly EF's words. But I have a good ear for voice, and in reconstructing how she spoke, I hope that I do not caricature her. I probably paid more attention to what she said and how she spoke than I did to anyone else in my life, before or since. Maybe at the start of both my marriages; but then, as EF had just advised, "Passion may mislead us furiously."

The ease with which she talked about the life of the heart, and included it naturally in a course of "Culture and Civilisation," made her a target for satire in the first weeks of term. Boys—even thirty-year-old men—being always boys, there were whispers and guffaws.

"Guess what? Her handbag fell open and there was a James Bond novel inside."

"I saw her being picked up last week in an E-Type Jag. Driven by a woman!"

"Took old Liz out last night and showed her a good time. Had a drink or two, quick bite, down a club, turns out she's a hot dancer, then back to her place, she gets out her stash, rolls us a couple of joints, and then"—whereupon a smirk might cross the boy-man's face—"and then, no, sorry, a gentleman never tells." As you may imagine, there were other, more baroque versions in which a gentleman did indeed tell.

Such reactions came from those uncertain how to deal with her poise, and disconcerted by her authority. Their fantasies may have been misconceived; but at the same time there *was* something racy about Elizabeth Finch. If not actual and present, then potential. And when I set my own mind to wander, it might easily throw up an image of EF, say, in a first-class sleeping compartment on a train crossing a darkened landscape; standing at the window in silk pyjamas, stubbing out a last cigarette, while a mysterious and now unidentifiable companion lets out a soft nasal whistle from the upper couchette. Outside, beneath a gibbous moon, she might discern a canted French vineyard or the dull shimmer of an Italian lake.

Of course, such fantasies define the fantasisers more than their subject. Either they presumed a glamorous past, or an imaginary present in which she sought compensation for the life she actually had; and further presumed that, like everybody else, she was needy and dissatisfied in some way. But this was not the case. The Elizabeth Finch who stood before us was the finished article, the sum of what she had made herself, what others had helped her make, and what the world had provided. The world not just in its contemporary manifestations but also in its long history. Gradually, we understood, and cast aside our clumsy musings as early, otiose reactions to her uniqueness. And without appearing to make any effort, she subdued us all. No, that's not quite right: it went deeper. Rather, she obliged us—simply by example—to seek and find within ourselves a centre of seriousness.

Linda came to seek my advice. This isn't something that often happens to me: I don't appear to be the counselling type. And as it turned out, she wanted to ask my advice about asking EF for *her* advice. I deliberately didn't quiz her, because with Linda it was bound to be some emotional drama. Besides, I thought approaching EF was a bad idea. She might be willing to discuss Goethe's love life in class, but that didn't mean she would be able, or willing, or even permitted by the college to give a student advice outside the lecture room. But I soon realised that Linda didn't really want my input; or rather, she wanted my input as long as it coincided with what she'd already decided to do. Some people are like that; perhaps most. So, to make her feel better, I shifted my position and approved her intention.

A day or two later, I was sitting by myself in the student bar when she appeared and sat down opposite.

"EF was wonderful," Linda began, already welling up. "I told her my heart trouble, and she was very understanding. She put out her hand and put it down like this close to where I was." Linda now did the same, laying her hand palm-down on the table. "And she told me that love is all there is. It's the only thing that matters." And then she—Linda, that is—burst into tears.

I'm not at my best in situations like this, so I said, "I'll get us another drink."

When I got back from the bar, she was gone. All she left behind was a damp palm-print halfway across the table, where she had laid her hand in imitation of Elizabeth Finch. I sat there and thought about Linda, probably for the first time. And the fact that EF never patronised even her most blurted opinions made me think about her more seriously as well. There was something urgent in Linda's glance when she looked at you. Urgent about what? Or just urgent generally? But as the imprint of her palm died, so did my concentration on her.

◆

"One hundred and seven years ago, this very spring, a great painter is waiting for death; not immediately, but soon. He knows it—he has known this would be his end since the final stage of the disease declared itself. He is already con-fined to a wheelchair. Tertiary syphilis presents in many punitive ways, but he has at least been spared what for a painter would have been the most punitive: blindness. Each morning, they bring him a large bunch of fresh flowers in a crystal vase. He takes pleasure in arranging them. On some mornings, he merely looks at them, imagining them into paint. On better days, rearrangement is followed by depiction. He works quickly, for obvious reasons.

"He is capturing the evanescent, holding on to that moment before cut flowers begin to fade. By cutting them, we make them die sooner; by painting them we preserve them long after they have been thrown out. At which point the art becomes the reality, and the original flowers merely brief, forgotten simulacra.

"We might consider what he might have been considering. For instance, that old question which has become known as the Mozart dilemma: is life beautiful, but sad; or sad, but beautiful? Or maybe he found an answer to bypass the question. Such as this: life is beautiful, *tout court*.

"On the other hand, you might condemn such imaginings as both fanciful and sentimental. I await your judgement."

All of a sudden, her trail of words had stopped, and the questions were returned to us. Yes, what *did* we think? And soon we were discussing whether art was a depiction of reality, a concentration of it, a superior substitute for it, or just a beguiling irrelevance. And Geoff was demanding to know the social and political purpose of painting a jug of flowers. Many of us merely repeated our already formulated opinions, or quoted pet lines once again ("Poetry makes nothing happen" versus "We are the movers and shakers / Of the world forever, it seems"); some of us actually began, in real time, to think for ourselves. You could watch it happening. And if, in retrospect, I acknowledge what EF would have seen at the time—that in many cases, "thinking for yourself" resulted less in truer, deeper thought than in the replacement of one *idée reçue* by another—even so, the process was to be valued for its own sake.

I never had one of those favourite, well-remembered schoolmasters when I was a boy, one who showed me the excitements of mathematics, or poetry, or botany, and perhaps interfered with me sexually at the same time. So I was the more grateful—though the word is insubstantial compared to the reality—for having met and known Elizabeth Finch. As she said, we must always consider the element of chance in our lives. I don't know what the average allotment of good luck in a life is or should be—it's an unanswerable question, and doubtless there is no "should" in it anyway—but I do know that she was part of my good luck.

Years later, over lunch, I asked her about the so-called Mozart dilemma. Is life sad but beautiful, or beautiful but sad? I felt, as I sat across from her with two plates of the day's pasta between us, as if I were consulting the oracle. "Life is both necessary, and unavoidable," she replied. I think she was telling me that the famous question was no more than a beguiling delusion. Or maybe not.

I never knew anyone with less self-pity than Elizabeth Finch. She would have considered self-pity vulgar—an adjective she only ever used in a moral, never a social, sense. As for herself, the lack of self-pity was part of the stoicism with which she faced life. She had known—and here I am only partly guessing—romantic disappointment, loneliness, the betrayal of friends, even a public shaming (which we'll come to in due course), but she faced them with calm indifference. "Faced" might suggest a facade, or at least a strategy; but her stoicism went to the core of her being. For EF, it was the only mental—and temperamental—approach to life. She bore pain implacably, and she never asked for help—moral help, that is. She once quoted to us, at dictation speed, words which I find in one of my student notebooks:

Some things are up to us and some are not up to us. Our opinions are up to us, and our impulses, desires, aversions—in short, whatever is our own doing. Our bodies are not up to us, nor are our possessions, our reputations, or our public offices, or, that is, whatever is not our doing. The things that are up to us are by nature free, unhindered, and unimpeded; the things that are not up to us are weak, enslaved, hindered, not our own. So remember, if you think that things naturally enslaved are free or that things not your own are your own, you will be thwarted, miserable and upset, and will blame both gods and men. But if you think that only what is yours is yours, and that what is not your own is, just as it is, not your own, then no one will ever coerce you, no one will hinder you, you will blame no one, you will not accuse anyone, you will not do a single thing unwillingly, you will have no enemies, and no one will harm you, because you will not be harmed at all.

I imagine that when she first read Epictetus, she found his truths self-evident rather than revelatory.

When I tell people that she was the most grown-up person I have known, I suppose what I mean is that there were principles very close behind, if not actually embedded in, all her actions and thoughts. Whereas for me—for most people— our principles have a more glancing effect on what we do and what we say.

We tend to associate romanticism with optimism, don't we? She, I think, was a romantic pessimist.

Here's another thing: the dead can't tell you that you are wrong. Only the living can do that—and they may be lying. So I trust the dead more. Is that bizarre, or is it sensible?

And further to this: why should we expect our collective memory—which we call history—to be any less fallible than our personal memory?

"We must always bear in mind what might have happened but didn't, as well as what did. Why, you might enquire—what happened, happened, and that's what we have to deal with. Perhaps not. And this is not just a jolly game of counterfactuals—what if Stauffenberg's bomb had killed Hitler?—it is also a serious enquiry. We are too apt, I would propose, to see history as a kind of Darwinism. The survival of the fittest, by which, of course, Darwin didn't mean the strongest or even the cleverest, merely those best equipped to adapt to changing circumstances. But it is not like this in actual human history. Those who survive, or excel, or overmaster are merely those who are better organised and wave bigger guns; those who are better at killing. Peaceable nations are rarely victorious—in ideas, to be sure, but ideas rarely prevail unless backed by the muzzle of a gun. It is lamentable, we would all agree, but it would be indolent not to recognise it. Because otherwise we merely have to sit on our hands—sit on our brains as well, and admit, To the victor the spoils, which also means, To the victor the truth.

"Do we really think that, say, the Etruscans were inferior to the Romans? Would they not have been a better influence on the world? Can we not see that the Albigensian heresy was more enlightened and more just than the medieval Church of Rome which crushed it so ruthlessly? Do we imagine that all those white settlers who exterminated all those indigenous tribes across the world were morally superior to their victims? Consider also that what we used to call the Dark Ages are now recognised as being full of Light. Consider the cases of the two Julians—two conspicuous examples of what might have been. Julian the Apostate, the last pagan emperor of Rome, who attempted to turn back the disastrous flood tide of Christianity. And the lesser-known Julian of Eclanum, who was relaxed, not to say celebratory, about the sexual instinct—indeed, reverential, since he thought it natural, and therefore implanted by God. Furthermore—and even more gravely in the eyes of the Church—he did not subscribe to the doctrine of original sin. The Church, you will recall, required—and still requires—the ceremony of baptism in order to purge the babe of original, and necessarily inherited, sin. Julian of Eclanum did not believe that God intended this to be the case. Alas, he lost out to St. Augustine, who affirmed and insisted upon the notion of an eternal taint handed down the generations, and therewith, an unassuageable guilt about sex. Imagine the consequences of this doctrinal dispute and imagine what the world would have been had Augustine not prevailed."

Elizabeth Finch paused, and read the minds of some of her students. "And no, I do not think it would have been like what are humorously termed the Swinging Sixties."

This class resulted in a rather less high-minded discussion in the bar afterwards, with a facetious exchange of squalid episodes. But this was in the second term, and our little group, as often happens, was beginning to fracture. From my own point of view, Geoff was becoming a bore, and I was tired of what I saw as his ritual animus against EF. There was also something awkward between Linda and myself, which I couldn't fathom: as far as I could ascertain, it was one of those cases where A confides in B, and then blames B for having accepted the confidence. Something like that? And then there was a third factor: Anna.

She was Dutch, as I think I said. About five foot four, with hair cut short and flat across her head, a variety of anoraks, and a way of looking at you which wasn't exactly challenging, but suggested that you might want to raise your game a little when talking to her; and that if you did, she would both note and appreciate it. I was between marriages (though obviously I wouldn't have put it like that at the time), a weekend father still being reminded by minor jibes and manipulations of why I was no longer married. I wasn't especially looking for anyone or anything. I liked women as friends. Particularly when they didn't manipulate me in any way. Particularly when they expected more of me—in an unthreatening way—and were Dutch.

Anna once told me that the first time she'd seen the phrase "casual sex" in English, she thought it was a misprint.

"How's that?"

"The S and the U."

I still didn't get it.

"Causal sex."

"What's that?"

"Sex for a cause."

"Isn't sex always for a cause? Even if the cause is, well, the cause of having sex?"

"I thought it meant sex for a reason other than the reason of just having sex. Sex for a cause, a greater purpose. Sex because you are in love, obviously, or sex because you want to explore the world. Sex because your country's population is in decline."

Sex as travel? Sex as civic duty? I thought, somehow, this was very Dutch. Also, sort of adorable.

We moved softly into a kind of complicity, drinking after class with one another rather than the group; a movie, a walk, an art gallery, a bookshop; simple small steps.

A few weeks of this, and I said, our heads close together, "Do you think it might be a good idea to have causal sex with one another?"

She turned her face to mine. "Is that a misprint?"

"No."

"Well, only if you really mean it."

I said that I did, even if I wasn't sure what I was signing up to.

Elizabeth Finch didn't view classes as discrete allotments of time in which a set amount of information was to be conveyed, discussed and settled upon. She liked us to continue processing the ideas she had laid before us. So our time together became more free-form, more open-ended.

"You mentioned monocultures," Geoff said a few weeks after she'd given us her mono-list. "I can't see what you've got against them. They're surely a sign of efficiency, of successful central planning."

"They might appear so," she replied, "and their advantages seem seductive. But let us go back to what we rather patronisingly call the good old days, when most people travelled small distances; often they never left the village in their entire lives, except for going to market in a nearby town. They saw a few people from outside—travellers, pedlars with gaudy goods, recruiting officers, brigands and so on. They were self-sufficient, and obliged to be; they stored food against hard winters. They were not independent: there was governance over them, of course—the priest, the magistrate, the squire. I do not sentimentalise: they could be cruel masters. No one should believe in Merrie England and suchlike tomfoolery. But life continued like this for centuries.

"Then the railways arrived, all over Europe. And what was their main function? It was, as both Ruskin and Flaubert pointed out, to allow people to get from A to B so that they could be equally stupid with one another in a different location. I paraphrase their words. It was widely assumed that technological advance would bring moral benefit; the railways brought none. Any more than the Internet is going to. No moral benefit at all. Nor do I mean an increase in immorality; rather, such technological wonders are morally neutral. A railway train could bring food to the famine-struck; equally, it could bring cannon, and cannon fodder, more quickly to the front.

"But you asked about monoculture. Let us begin with the word in its agricultural sense. Those old enclosed villages and towns produced the food, the clothes, the goods they required. The railway brought different food and clothes and goods at different prices. Very quickly—and since the law of the market is also morally neutral—they found they could buy more cheaply things they had traditionally produced themselves. And so, the countryside became increasingly monocultural. Take those charming Provençal villages and towns. All of a sudden, wine cost less when produced elsewhere; contrarily, their grain might be worth more if sent to another region. They ceased to be self-sufficient. And so when the vineyards were struck by phylloxera or the fields by blight or hurricane, the neighbourhood starved. And became dependent upon the goodwill or the self-interest of others. Who might have been distracted or negligent or, indeed, actively hostile. I tell you nothing you do not know."

She often overestimated us like this; it was flattering. In retrospect, it may have been knowing and calculated; but it was still flattering.

"And then we may take a wider view of the term 'monoculture.' The monoculture of nations. The old nation states of Europe and beyond—what defined them? Race and geography, of course; conquest and empire; also, insane ideas about purity and exceptionalism. Remember that line from the 'Marseillaise,' and I translate: 'Let an impure blood sluice through the furrows of our fields.' Purity, blood. Plus religion, of course, and all the competing monocultures therein. I happened to be reading *Hitler's Table Talk* the other evening, and as he puts it, there are—or were—one hundred and seventy important religions in the world, all of which claimed to be the sole repositories of the truth. One hundred and sixty-nine of them must therefore be in error."

Geoff, who was always alert and suspicious when EF approached anything political, asked, "Are you putting Hitler on our reading list?"

"You will remember," replied EF calmly, "that my list was entirely optional. The course of each lesson will, I hope, suggest to you certain books with which you are unfamiliar and that you might wish to read."

"But are you suggesting," Geoff continued, with a touch of aggression, "that we read Hitler?"

"I am suggesting that we familiarise ourselves with those who oppose us and whom we oppose, whether it be a living or a dead figure, whether it be a religious or political opponent, or even a daily newspaper or weekly magazine. Know thy enemy—it is a simple and cogent rule—even thy dead enemy, for he may easily resuscitate. Also, as a great writer once put it, 'These monsters explain history to us.'"

But Geoff would not give up. "My dad was killed in the war and you're telling me to read Hitler?"

It was the only time I saw Elizabeth Finch lose her composure. And yet—and of course—she did it her way. She turned very slightly, until she was facing Geoff, and replied: "I am sorry for your loss. But—without in any way wishing to pull rank—I think we would find that Hitler destroyed far more of my family than he did of yours. That will be all for today."

And she walked out, picking her handbag from the lectern as she passed. No one wanted to be the first to speak. Eventually, more bewildered than belligerent, Geoff said,

"How was I to know she was Jewish?"

None of us answered.

I can't say that we ever attained the Socratic ideal she invoked in her first address to us; but we felt ourselves being drawn out, able to exercise our intelligence, able to theorise without fear of scorn. Not that she dealt in theory (or, for that matter, scorn); the nearest she got was a kind of epigrammatic generalisation. If I say that she used charm and wit in her teaching, that might make her sound manipulative, even knowingly seductive. Well, she *was* seductive, but not in any conventional way.

One evening, she was talking to us about Venice, and explaining a sequence of paintings by Carpaccio. She broke off:

"Of course, we should, all things being equal, be on the side of the underdog, the victim, the defeated, the obliterated, should we not?" She looked back up to the screen. "In the case of George and the Dragon—an encounter in which the dice were theologically loaded—any morally sentient human being must surely sympathise with the poor dragon."

We gazed at the painting, in which the lance of a heavily armoured George pierces the beast's mouth and exits through the back of his skull, while the pious princess, whom the future saint has come to rescue, prays on a rock behind him. The dragon, while fearsomely scaly, is in fact no bigger than the saint's horse.

"You might agree that this is more a demonstration of superior weaponry than of superior piety."

Geoff, always keen to stir, said, "But it's St. George—that's not very patriotic of you, if I may say so."

"You may indeed, Geoff. But please consider that there were many St. Georges, patron saints of many countries and cities, and that the desert landscape in which this encounter takes place is hardly the garden of England. The wider point is that our purpose here is to transcend mere patriotism. We might analyse the words of 'Land of Hope and Glory,' but we shall not be singing them."

Do you see what I mean? She was corrective but not diminishing, as she directed us elegantly away from the obvious.

"Consider too that the poor dragon who has been terrifying the city in the background—witness the dismembered body parts of previous victims in the foreground—is not just some extreme example of wildlife, one even scarier than those rogue elephants which run berserk in India. The dragon is symbolic. He lives in, and represents, Cappadocia, a pagan country until St. George arrived to demonstrate the power of muscular, or rather military, Christianity. And if we continue on with this spiritual storyboard, we shall see how the taming of the dragon leads directly to the conversion of the whole country to Christianity. So what Carpaccio gives us here is both a freeze-frame from an action movie and a compelling work of propaganda. One secret of the Christian religion's success was always to employ the best moviemakers."

If she taught us one thing, it was that history is for the long haul; further, that it is not something inert and comatose, lying there and waiting for us to apply a spyglass or telescope to it; instead, it is active, effervescent, at times volcanic. I suppose her "formative years," as they say, took place in the fifties, yet she no more embodied them than she embodied the Age of Enlightenment or the fourth century AD. Like some ancient goddess—yes, I know what I'm saying—she seemed to stand aside from time, or perhaps above it.

"I would like to suggest that failure can tell us more than success, and a bad loser more than a good loser. Further, that apostates are always more interesting than true believers, than holy martyrs. Apostates are the representatives of doubt, and doubt—vivid doubt—is the sign of an active intelligence. I have previously mentioned Julian the Apostate. Given who we are, we might take as our point of entry the poet Swinburne. Algernon Charles Swinburne, himself an apostate in revolt against Victorian values. Though it has to be said, a melodramatic, even hysterical one. Another example of the English public schoolboy marked in both senses by the cruel, yet to some enjoyable, practice of flagellation. He pursued traditional British paths of dissolution, from which he was rescued by the lesser poet Theodore Watts-Dunton, who took him to live soberly at The Pines, number 11 Putney Hill, Putney, a semidetached suburban villa. Fate can be such an ironist, would you not agree? The reformed sinner was of course a well-used Victorian trope—and none the better for it. But I am a little astray.

"Swinburne in his poem 'Hymn to Proserpine' has the following memorable couplet:

Thou hast conquered, O pale Galilean; the world has
    grown grey from thy breath;
We have drunken of things Lethean, and fed on the ful-
    ness of Death.

The pale Galilean is of course Jesus of Nazareth, and that phrase was supposedly uttered by Julian the Apostate as he lay dying on the battlefield. Famous last words admitting the victory of Christianity over paganism. And indeed, Julian turned out to be the last pagan emperor. What the papers—the pagan newspapers at least—might have called a 'hold-out hero.' He was a scholar-soldier: when he set off to campaign in Gaul, the empress Eusebia gave him a library so that he could philosophise between battles. Strangely Swinburne does not name him. He names, however, in the poem's title, Proserpine, who in the ancient world was, among other things—the gods being famous multitaskers—Goddess and Defender of Rome. She was now about to be replaced by a different protectress: Mary the mother of Christ, who has presided over that city ever since.

"We might conceive that Julian's words are meant to be read as a gracious concession of spiritual defeat. Julian the good loser. Not a bit of it. Swinburne, like many distinguished predecessors, is identifying this as the moment when European history and civilisation took a calamitous wrong turn. The old gods of Greece and Rome were gods of light and joy; men and women understood that there was no other life, so that light and joy had to be found here, before nothingness encloses us. Whereas these new Christians obeyed a

God of darkness, of pain and servitude; one who declared that light and joy existed only after death in His confected heaven, progress towards which was filled with sorrow, guilt and fear. 'We have fed on the fulness of Death,' indeed. On such matters, both Julian and Swinburne agreed.

"Of course," EF went on, "we should always seek to avoid self-pity. To imagine that it all went wrong in the Persian desert in AD 363, and sixteen centuries later we discover at birth that we have been dealt a hand stacked against us, allowing us to cry, 'It's not my fault, Guv.' It is better to believe that everyone else feels like this, and that a stacked hand is normal. Historical self-pity is no more attractive than personal self-pity."

Of which no one could accuse Elizabeth Finch.

Another of her techniques was to start a class just by asking what we knew about a particular subject. These could be scary moments. What *did* we know about whatever? We were hardly experts on anything. Yet her approach was encouraging: "There are no wrong answers, even if all the answers are wrong." This was how she put it when announcing the subject of that particular day: "Slavery and its abolition."

I shall amalgamate our answers. William Wilberforce, father of Soapy Sam. Harriet Beecher Stowe. The Thirteenth Amendment, Abraham Lincoln. Slave traders in Africa who first sold slaves to the British for transportation. Some traders were African, some Arab. Slave-owning common throughout the world. The Royal Navy patrolling the high seas, stop-and-search vessels enforcing the anti-slavery laws. Slave owners compensated for losing their "property," no compensation for having been a slave (Geoff).

"Yes," said EF. "Very good." By which she meant our answers were roughly what she expected. A few dates, please. Date of Thirteenth Amendment. No? 1865. Declaration of Independence. Yes, 1776. Date when the Pilgrim Fathers landed at Plymouth Rock? A little eager discussion, as among students at a college quiz night. 1620, very good. A final question: date when the first slaves were brought to an English colony, landing at the ironically named Point Comfort? No? Still no? She paused. "1619."

She said no more for the moment, leaving us to our own reflections and calculations: for instance, that slaves and the British arrived together, and the British held slaves on that continent for almost twice as long as Americans did.

"Which brings me to the wider point." With EF, there always was one. "Ernest Renan, the great nineteenth-century French historian and philosopher, once wrote the following: 'Getting its history wrong is part of being a nation.' Note, if you please, what he did not say. He did not say, 'Getting its history wrong is part of becoming a nation.' This would also be a true remark, but one considerably less provocative. We are familiar with the foundation myths on which countries rely, and which they furiously propagate. Myths of heroic struggle against an occupying power, against the tyranny of aristocracy and Church, struggles which produced martyrs whose spilt blood waters the delicate plant of liberty. But Renan is not talking about this. He says that getting its history wrong is part of *being* a nation. In other words, in order to believe in what we think our nation stands for, we must constantly, every day, in small acts or thoughts and large, deceive ourselves, as we constantly rehearse our comforting bedtime stories. Myths of racial and cultural superiority. Belief in benign monarchs, infallible popes, and honest government. Assumptions that the religion into which you are born, or have chosen to adopt, just happens to be the one sect which is true among hundreds of heathen creeds and apostasies out there.

"And this disjunction between who we are and who we believe we are leads naturally to the question of national hypocrisy, of which the British are a famous example. Famous, that is, in the eyes of others who are inevitably blinded by their own national hypocrisies."

Strangely, it was after this class that Anna and I had our first row. For once, we stayed with our group in the student bar. Which made it public, and so more corrosive. And she began it.

"All I'm saying is, I don't feel personally responsible."

"But you had an empire as well, you had slaves."

"So did every other European country. Even focking Belgium."

I laughed at the wonky vowel which at other times I would have found endearing.

"They were the worst, Belgium," I agreed. "Conrad. *Heart of Darkness*."

"But I'm not a focking Belgian anyway."

"Well, don't you think there's such a thing as collective responsibility?"

"Yes," Geoff interrupted, "like with the German people as led by Elizabeth Finch's favourite diarist."

This intervention annoyed both of us.

"I do not feel, and am not, responsible for what the soldiers and merchants of my country did centuries before I was born. And when my ancestors were the equivalent of slaves in one of the poorest parts of Holland."

"A) Your ancestors weren't slaves, bought and sold and

raped and tortured and killed on a whim. And B) Isn't it up to the descendants of slaves to tell us whether they feel that a terrible crime was committed against their ancestors, the pain of which is still with them?"

"Go for it, Neil, we'll make a lefty of you yet."

"Fuck off, Geoff."

But I didn't look at him. I looked only at Anna. The others were silent.

"You can't *make* me feel responsible. Or guilty. I'm not. Sorry. That's that."

"I'm not trying to make you do or be anything. You are what you are."

"Thanks for reminding me. Thanks for allowing me to be myself. What's that thing your sainted Elizabeth Finch likes to quote? 'Some things ...'"

Christ, now *she* was attacking EF as well. "Some things are up to us and some are not up to us. Epictetus."

"I know it's focking Epictetus. So what I'm saying is that Dutch slavery, of which I expect you know very little, is not up to me, and you can't make it so."

"I wasn't trying to."

"Of course you were."

We left, our drinks unfinished, and went our separate ways. Maybe all quarrels are really about something else, as they say. But in retrospect, it was a turning point.

At the end of our year with Elizabeth Finch, we were asked to submit an essay. It was to be of our own devising, but could—indeed, should—relate to a subject arising from our time together. I remember her adding, wryly, "And you may show your workings if you so wish." We didn't discuss it much, perhaps fearing ideas theft. While EF's way of teaching excited us, it also laid clear how few original thoughts our own brains were producing.

I failed to turn anything in. I mooched scrappily around with a few vast notions—the frailty of historical truth, the frailty of human character, the frailty of religious belief, and so on—but I can't remember writing more than a paragraph or two. What was taking up my attention instead was the frailty of human relations and the frailty of marriage. I'd been divorced now for a couple of years, and was discovering that the notion of a clean, legal break is delusional. Hurt, resentment, financial suffering—they all continue. And it's easy for the sanest human being to become obsessive, revengeful, self-pitying—insane, in other words—often prompted by a simple lawyer's letter, a single session with a new therapist, or a supposedly adult discussion about the future of a child. I'll spare you the details, because I want to spare myself the details.

I went to EF and explained, as best I could, how my brain, as well as a slice of my heart, had absconded in the recent weeks.

"I'm sorry," I said in conclusion. "I feel I've let you down."

I somehow expected her to console me. Instead, she said quietly, "I'm sure it is only temporary."

Solipsistically, I thought she was referring to my post-divorce crisis. Later, I realised she was referring to my letting her down, and to that being temporary. That somehow, in the future, I would justify her belief in me. This often happened: she said things, you didn't understand them, but remembered them, and years later they made sense.

I am not a bold person. Those decisions in my life which might be mistaken for boldness (marrying, divorcing, having a child out of wedlock, living abroad for a while) would be better ascribed to either nervous overexcitement or coward-ice. If, in our lives, as the philosopher decreed, some things are up to us and some are not up to us, and freedom and happiness depend upon recognising the difference between the two categories, then my life has been the opposite of philosophi-cal. I have seesawed and zigzagged between thinking myself in control and realising that everything was hopeless and way beyond me, both the understanding and the living. Well, like most people, I suppose.

I had failed EF. I had been asked to do one thing by her and had failed. She had been forgiving in a way particular to her. She had not made me feel bad. So as I turned to go, I stopped, and in a moment of nervous overexcitement (caused by the fear I might never see her again), found myself saying, without looking at her,

"This may be quite out of order . . ."

"Yes?"

"But would you . . . I mean . . . might we have a drink sometime . . . or even . . . lunch?"

Now I looked at her, and she was smiling.

"My dear Neil, of course. And lunch, I think, would be the more enjoyable."

And so another part of my life began. We would meet twice or three times a year, at a small Italian restaurant in West London, near where she lived. The rules were clear, without ever really being explained. I would arrive promptly at one; she would be sitting there, smoking. We would have the pasta of the day, a green salad, one glass of white wine and black coffee. Once, early on, I went off-piste and ordered the veal escalope. "How is that?" she asked, leaning eagerly across the table. "Disappointing?" Lunch would last seventy-five minutes; she would always pay. As I sat down, she would say,

"And what have you got for me?" putting the initial onus on me; but that was all right. And because I knew I had only seventy-five minutes with her, it concentrated not just my choice of subject, but also, in a way—no, absolutely—my intelligence. I was cleverer in her presence. I knew more, I was more cogent; and I was desperate to please her.

As I said, she was not in any way a public person; nor would she have wanted to be. She had neither the temperament nor the aptitude for fame. I doubt it was a matter she ever considered. I remember her once remarking that Clio was the Greek muse of history, usually portrayed with a book or scroll in her hand, "whereas in our more enlightened age the Clio Awards are distributed in the United States for excellence in advertising." Also, that Clio was the muse of lyre playing, but doubted that those showing excellence in advertising would be serenaded by a bank of lyre players. Her manner was droll and wry, and thus—to us, anyway—neither patronising nor snobby. It was also a way of saying: don't be taken in by the proclaimed values of your own age.

I asked her, during one of our lunches, why she preferred teaching adults.

"I am not excited by incuriosity," she replied. "Paradoxically, the young are more certain of themselves, while their ambitions, if objectively nebulous to the outsider, seem clear and achievable to them. Whereas with adults . . . it's true that some enrol as a kind of self-indulgence but most come because they feel a lack in their lives, a sense that they might have missed something, and that they now have a chance—perhaps even a final chance—to put things right. And I find that profoundly affecting."

I thought back to how the class had first reacted to her: with a certain awe, much preliminary silence and awkwardness, some unspoken amusement, all quickly replaced by a genuine warmth. Also, by a kind of protectiveness, because in a way we sensed that she was unfit for the world, and that her high-mindedness might make her vulnerable. And this was not meant to be patronising either.

I also realised—later on—that the way she had described her adult students applied exactly and absolutely to my case; which was doubtless why I wanted to hang on to her after I had taken my degree. Also, perhaps, why she allowed me to.

I would sometimes bend to please her; she would never modify a thought or opinion to avoid disagreement. I got used to this—I had to. Once, we were talking about public reaction to some political scandal, and I suggested that it was normal for people to need someone to blame.

"Normal doesn't mean it's a good idea," she answered.

"But if there's someone you can blame, then you can do something about it."

"Like what?"

"Vote them out of office."

"It's a recurrent delusion that a change of government will make a difference."

"That's a counsel of despair."

"No, it's a counsel of realism. Do you see me despairing?"

"No. But I also bet you have voted in every single election."

"In the sure knowledge that it will effect little."

"Then why do it?"

"Civic duty. It is expected."

At which point I slightly lost it. "That sounds incredibly patronising."

"To whom?"

"To . . . well, the rest of the electorate."

"You mean that I am meant to share fully in their hopes and dreams and subsequent disappointments? A politician's main function is to disappoint."

"And that sounds incredibly cynical, you know."

"I disagree. I am not a cynic."

"What are you then?"

"I am not vain enough to attach a label to myself."

She was, as ever, preternaturally calm. Which sometimes unnerved me. Was she just toying with me? Still teaching me?

"So you're not a cynic. Are you . . . an anarchist?"

"Intellectually, I see the attraction. Realistically, it would never work, given the crooked timber of humanity."

"So you accept that we need some organising power?"

"I accept that we shall have one, willy-nilly."

"And that constitutional democracy is the least worst system we've so far discovered?"

"It would have been a democrat who said that, wouldn't it?"

"So you're not a cynic or an anarchist. Are you . . . an Epicurean?"

"He was certainly a very wise psychologist."

"I think you're a Stoic."

"It is indeed an attractive position."

"Because it lets you off the hook?"

"My dear Neil, you're getting a little close to insult."

"I'm sorry. I . . ."

"Oh, I wasn't in the least offended. I was just pointing out how insults most often occur when an argument is being lost. And you are trying to stick labels on me. I am not a steamer trunk."

Undaunted, I gave it a last try. "OK, then, well, are you a feminist?"

She smiled at me. "Naturally—I am a woman."

You see how hard it was to have a straightforward conversation with her? No, that's another insult, I realise. I mean: you see how hard it was for me, and those like me, ever to be in charge of a conversation with her, or even be on equal terms? Not because she manipulated it—she was the least manipulative woman I've ever met—but because she examined things more widely, with a different horizon and focus.

You can see, I hope, why I adored her. And I adored the fact that she was much cleverer than me. When I put this—in so many words—to Anna, she called me an intellectual masochist. And I didn't mind *that* label either.

A question worth asking, even at this late stage. At first I thought Elizabeth Finch a Romantic pessimist; now I would call her a Romantic Stoic. Are the two conditions compatible? Can they coexist, or is one the consequence of the other? It's tempting to posit that EF started off as a high-minded Romantic, and then, after life had inflicted its inevitable disappointments on her, she became a Stoic. Not that I had any actual evidence. But what if it turned out that she was once engaged to be married, but was jilted when on the way to the registry office? Or one might imagine a long infatuation followed by sudden betrayal and violent disillusionment. Such a narrative might offer a logical, indeed "natural," explanation, but it would also, psychologically, be banal; and banality was rarely a key when it came to EF. I prefer to believe that, as her heart and mind developed she became a Romantic and a Stoic in parallel. Uncommon, implausible? Yes, but so was she.

My affair with Anna lasted a year and more, then succumbed to its inbuilt asymmetry. Those characteristics which first attracted us to one another—her intensity, my calmness—came to be seen differently: as melodrama on the one hand, emotional indolence on the other. No real harm was done—though that is what one accused of emotional indolence would say, I suppose. But we were fond of one another and stayed so.

I didn't at first tell her about my lunches with EF because—well, because. Some friends we are possessive of, others not. But one day, I mentioned it, since I was seeing EF shortly. Anna didn't seem particularly interested as I described what it was like, how it was structured, where we met, what she ate and drank.

"That must be nice for you," said Anna. "For both of you."

"Yes. It's something special."

"So why didn't you tell me about it before?"

"Oh well, I don't know. Some things you keep to yourself, don't you?"

"*You* do," she replied with a familiar edge to her tone. But I wasn't responsible for her emotions any more, so I changed the subject.

Two days later, EF was just finishing her pasta when a chair was pulled up to our table.

"Mind if I join you?" said Anna, joining us anyway.

"Anna, how very pleasant," said EF calmly, as if this sort of intervention was always happening to her, and always welcome.

"I just thought it would be good to see you again. You look very well."

"Thank you, Anna. And so do you."

A few more meaningless niceties were exchanged, and EF rose to her feet.

"I'll leave you two together." After a brief consultation with Antonio, she left the restaurant without looking back.

"What the *fuck* do you think you're up to?"

"Wanted to set eyes on her again. It's a free country, isn't it?"

"Not always."

At which point, Antonio came over. "Signora Finch says order what you like, she will pay for it all tomorrow."

I was furious, yet embarrassed by my anger. Anna reacted as if I was being absurdly possessive and tight-arsed, whereas she was remaining her normal, warm, spontaneous self. Furthermore, she made it sound as if her relationship with EF was somehow as valid as mine. At least I restrained myself from saying "Don't ever do that again," or "So there *is* such a thing as a free lunch." Instead, I just sulked, and she futilely tried to tease me about sulking, which I futilely denied, and . . . oh, you know how it goes, don't you?

I wrote EF a letter, apologising and explaining that Anna's arrival had nothing to do with me (though I suppose it had). In reply, I got a brief note making no comment on anything I'd said. She merely wrote: "We shall continue the conversation." Which we did, to my great relief.

Our lunches continued for nearly twenty years, a still and radiant point in my life. She would propose a date; I would always make myself free. As she got older—well, as we both got older—she was beset by the usual ailments and mishaps, of which she always made light. But to me she was unchanged: in dress, conversation, appetite (small), smoking (determined).

I would arrive, she would already be there, I would sit down, and she would ask, "So what have you got for me?" And I would smile, and do my best to gratify her curiosity, to make her laugh, to report from a world of failed marriages, successful children and a peripatetic career. Her intellectual interests were timeless. And she always paid for lunch.

She cancelled, or rather deferred, twice in a row, "given the unforeseen yet unignorable depredations of the human envelope," as she put it both times. I failed to understand that she was dying. There was no farewelling, no summons, no final message. I imagined that she had died uncomplainingly, stoically, in silence, almost in secret. I received an invitation to the funeral from one Christopher Finch, apparently her brother; until this moment I had always assumed she was an only child. Some thirty of us assembled in the smaller chapel of a chilly brick crematorium in South London. There was Bach on a CD, readings from Donne and Gibbon, then the brother spoke some simple, touching words, mainly about their childhood; he looked at the coffin and wept. I recognised a few faces and nodded at them, shook hands with Christopher Finch on the way out, and declined to go on to an upstairs room in a nearby pub, where there would be sandwiches and wine. Somehow, I wasn't ready to discuss her with others, ask the conventional questions and get the conventional answers. Also to observe, as a wake progresses, how voices become raised, how awkward laughter starts, spreads, then becomes raucous. Laughter which means well, we're still alive today, and Liz wouldn't disapprove, would she— no killjoy, that's one thing you can say about our Liz. Why, do you remember when … No, none of that. I also wanted to avoid those moments of competitive grief, always a danger on such occasions. Who knew her best, who mourned her most. I wanted Elizabeth Finch to myself, and so I took her home in my head.

A lawyer's letter informed me that Elizabeth Finch had left me "all my papers and my library, to do with as he wishes." I was flattered but baffled. The two books she had written were long out of print. The dreamer in me wondered if she had left some sudden, late masterpiece which I might have the honour of ushering into the world. The voyeur in me wondered if she had left a laceratingly self-revealing diary; at times, my tawdry imagination was no better than those of the loucher students she had taught. I somehow wanted there to be a secret to discover, even if it was no more than, say, a mild addiction to gambling on the horses. (EF in a betting shop! Or telephoning someone she might describe as "my turf accountant"!) But the sensible part of me judged all such suppositions improbable. I expected that EF, just as she had controlled her life, would also have controlled her posterity. There would probably be a brief, lucid note instructing me what to do.

I went to the block of red-brick flats in West London to which I had never previously been invited. It looked as if it had once had uniformed porterage; nowadays the porter was diminished to an entry code by the front door. Waiting for me was Christopher Finch, only sibling and sole executor. He was cheery, white-haired, pink-cheeked and plump in a short car coat, blue suit and quasi-regimental tie; seemingly as unexotic and unmysterious as his sister had been exotic and opaque.

"I don't really know what this is about," I said.

"Me neither. But then I'm not a literary chap in any way. Though I like a good yarn. Something to distract me."

"Yes, we all need that."

"Ah, but I read the sort of stuff my sister would have scorned."

"I think she was much less scornful than people assumed," I said, then felt I had gone too far. "Sorry—you were her brother."

"Yes, but you're not telling me she would have approved of Alistair MacLean, Desmond Bagley and Dick Francis."

"I wish I'd seen her trying to read one of them."

He chuckled. "Like you couldn't imagine her wolfing down a full English breakfast."

Her flat was immaculately tidy, beige and brown in tone, books and small prints on the wall, a heavy-shaded standard lamp. There was no television in the sitting room, and no microwave in the kitchen; just a tiny fridge, an antique gas range and a Baby Belling; on the floor a cardboard box filled with carrier bags. A single bed, fitted wardrobes, and an underpowered bedside light. There was no plant life anywhere. A very old portable record player stood on its side near a rack of LPs. The Roberts radio was original, not a vintage remake. Flats and houses left empty by death can often feel abandoned and depressing; it's normal, in our grief, to anthropomorphise such places. Yet somehow, this didn't apply here—perhaps because EF had never embraced and loved the place, merely occupied it. And in return the flat—how can I put this without more anthropomorphism?—felt indifferent, even superior to our presence.

I scanned the bookshelves. "A distinct shortage of Desmond Bagleys."

Christopher Finch laughed.

"When did you last see her? I mean, if I may . . ."

"A few days before she died. But before that it'd been a year and more. I'd come up to town every so often, and we'd have lunch. In a non-alcoholic tea shop. And as you can imagine, it wasn't easy getting her to come down and visit."

"Where do you . . . ?"

"Essex. Now that's a whole train journey away."

He said it ironically, but without resentment, merely an acknowledgement that this was how his sister was.

He went on, "I used to see her every few months. Less frequently as time went on."

"She was good at putting people off," I said. "Politely but firmly."

"That was my sister for you. She never told me she was ill until near the end. I suppose she wanted to keep it to herself."

We looked at one another. It was hard to imagine a more dissimilar brother and sister. They even had different ways of being well mannered.

"I suppose you'd better be about your business. I'll just check out the unlikely notion that there's some wine in the fridge."

An unlocked filing cabinet contained everything to do with banks, lawyers, accountants, house insurance and so on. Her will had been straightforward.

Her desk was an Arts and Crafts item in English oak, the only piece of furniture that was more than just functional. It too was unlocked. Files, notebooks, papers, typescripts.

"I'm not sure how to proceed," I said.

"Why don't you just take it all away? Anything that properly belongs to the family you can bring back."

It was nice to be trusted. I said I'd report in due course— perhaps I could take him to lunch.

"You could always come down to Essex," he replied. "It's only a train journey away."

"By the way, when did she make her will?"

"Oh, quite a while ago. Fifteen or twenty years? I can check for you."

"Yes, please."

We shook hands. I took the contents of her desk away with me. A week or so later, all her books, carefully boxed up, arrived in my flat.

For quite some months, they stayed in their boxes, while the contents of her desk went unexamined. It wasn't the weight of responsibility that held me back; more, superstition. Her body was gone, cremated according to her instructions; her memory, kept by family and friends and ex-students, would burn intermittently. But here, in my flat, was something between body and memory. Dead pieces of paper which were somehow capable of giving off life.

Tentatively, and with mixed moral feelings, I took out a few of her notebooks. They were squat, red-and-black hard-bound items, cheap imports from Flying Eagle of Shanghai. This surprised me: I would have expected elegant doeskin in subtle hues. But then I remembered the same kind of surprise when I found out what cheap cigarettes she elegantly stowed in her tortoiseshell case. The notebooks were numbered by EF; some were missing, and none was dated. Nor were they internally sequential; she clearly went back to add comments and corrections. They were written in a hand I would call bastardised italic; or personalised italic. Always in pencil, as if to say: all thought is provisional, and may be rubbed out. And her handwriting varied, though whether this was caused by age, tiredness or mood, I cannot guess.

I poured myself a glass of wine and let my eye dodge here and there.

—To be a stoic in an age of self-pity is to be judged standoff-ish; worse, unfeeling.

—The personal is political—such has been the mantra of the day for decades. An easy complaint. Rather, the personal is historical. (And the personal, lest we forget, is also hysterical.)

—Strange how there are men who convince themselves that lust is an emotion. Indeed, one of the primary ones.

—And there are many others who confuse feeling guilty with being absolved. They are less aware that there are stages in between.

—A woman described herself recently as "preternaturally truthful." Which is melodramatic nonsense. There are not degrees of truthfulness. There are degrees of lying, but that is another matter.

—"The philosophers are not agreed on the number of the passions." AC.

No, stop. I had barely started, and was already turning this into The Wit and Wisdom of Elizabeth Finch. She would have hated that: like another three-adjective misdescription. I'm anthologising her against her will. And I can't even be sure these are her own thoughts. That last one, for instance—about the number of the passions—is clearly by someone else.

And what about this: "The task of the present is to correct our understanding of the past. And that task becomes the more urgent when the past cannot be corrected." This might be EF's voice; equally, it could be a translation from some European philosopher-historian of the past two hundred years.

Some entries were paragraph-length, some page-length,

some attributed, many not. Some seemed scraps, or whimsi-calities:

—St. Sebastian//hedgehog.

Here, at the top of a page, all alone, were a pair of initials:

—PG

Wodehouse? Parental Guidance? PG Tips—perhaps her favourite brand of tea?

And here was another solitary entry at the top of a page:

—J, dead at thirty-one.

This intrigued me much more. Simple, plangent words. What had I said about the voyeur inside me? Unhesitatingly, I imagined a young man of particular interest to EF. I made him well formed, and taller than her. A cousin, perhaps, or a friend of Christopher's? Her first lover? But why did I imme-diately assume it was a man? In any case, someone she was deeply in love with. Definitely a few years older. And dead at thirty-one? A sudden rare cancer, a motorbike smash-up, drug overdose, perhaps even suicide. EF griefstruck, her heart paralysed, frozen for many years ... or, indeed, for ever?

I was shocked—mainly by the novelettish banality of what my freewheeling mind threw up. How embarrassed EF would have been by her disciple. And yet ...

A few days later, Christopher rang up.

"She made her will eighteen years ago. No codicils. A

simple probate, the solicitor assures me. Knowing them, that'll mean at least a year."

"Thank you. And may I ask ..." I didn't know how best to put it.

"Fire away."

"Well, this may sound a bit odd. But did she, as a young woman, have a friend called J?"

"Jay? As in J-A-Y?"

"No, no, just J the initial. I don't know what it stands for. Someone who would have known Elizabeth. Perhaps a friend of yours."

"Hmm, J's a pretty common initial. John, Jimmy, Jack. Well, there was my old pal Jack Martin, bit of a ladies' man. Always used to say, 'Never trust a man with two Christian names.' Ha ha. Now, did Jack know Liz? Well, I can phone him if you like."

"No, no, that's not necessary. The J I'm after died at the age of thirty-one. Do you remember anyone in your circle, or your family's circle ...?" I didn't like to add the possibility that it might have been a woman. It seemed a bit early in our acquaintance.

He thought for a bit. "There aren't many people you know who die at that age. There was Benson, of course, he must have been about thirty. Went out into the woods and hanged himself, poor devil."

"Did he know Elizabeth?"

"Oh no, he was part of, what shall I call it, a chaps' drinking club. And now I remember, his name was Toby."

"Well, if anything occurs to you ..."

"Yes, of course. Come down and see us sometime. It's only a train journey away."

★

From EF's notebooks:

—There can be a complacency to failure as much as a complacency to success.

Needless to say, she had neither. And I doubt she ever thought of herself in terms of success versus failure.

And me? My favourite child, Nell, aged thirteen, once said of me, "Dad is the King of Unfinished Projects." I smiled at the memory of this sudden truth; also, at the pleasure of being examined by a sharp-minded teenager. But was I being complacent—that's the question.

Do marriages count as "projects"? I suppose so, even if it rarely feels like that at the start. And both of mine went "unfinished" in the sense that they were terminated, if neither by me. As I said, I've had a lot of jobs, especially in what is now called the "hospitality sector"; I even half-owned a restaurant at one point. And if that went "unfinished" I would blame the economic recession of the time. I spent a year or so refurbishing vintage cars and selling them on. I have a lot of energy and enthusiasm; as an actor, I was a quick study. But I am often restless. I tried to educate myself above the level I was at when I left college, even if to the outsider (or wife) it merely looked as if I was reading a lot of books. Who knows, when my hair is white, I may even take up pottery; I hear it can be very satisfying.

But I don't regard all this chopping and changing as failure; nor do I feel complacent about it. What's the opposite of complacent? Guilt-ridden? Self-hating? Are such emotions meant to be proof of integrity? Of course I feel guilt about my marriages and accept, in both cases, approximately forty-five percent of the responsibility. But should I feel guiltier than that to avoid the label of complacency? Well, I doubt there are too many people interested in the answer to that question.

The strange thing was, that despite many invitations from Christopher, I never did get down to Essex. Perhaps I was unconsciously siding with his sister. But when he came up to town, I always made sure to take him to a restaurant which served wine. He had already put the flat on the market and received a couple of offers. In reply, I told him that his sister's papers were interesting, but had left me a little confused. He laughed sympathetically. I said that there might be something publishable there, but couldn't be sure. Privately, I thought a small book of aphorisms and observations, printed in a hundred copies, might be the way to go.

"Well, I leave it all to you. Elizabeth obviously trusted you, so I shall too."

I felt encouraged—by his straightforwardness as much as his promise.

"It's strange how differently the two of you turned out."

"That's putting it mildly."

"And your parents?"

"Somewhere in the middle. Which means that both of us disappointed them. Oh, not obviously, and I 'gave them grandchildren' as the saying goes. But I think they wanted Liz to be more conventional, and me to be more ... go-ahead, I suppose."

After school, he'd taken a short-service commission, then trained as an accountant. He ended up combining the two and doing the books for some regiment. I'd never thought about the army having accountants before.

"Safe," he said, as if in self-rebuke. "Safe."

"No one's ever called her Liz before," I commented.

"Used to call her that when we were kids, until she stopped me. I would have been about ten, so she must have been seven. Told me her name was Elizabeth. And I was Christopher, not Chris. Naturally, I obeyed her. But I've always called her Liz to myself. Massive rebellion, eh?"

"Were you close?"

"Hard to say. I was her big brother. Mum and Dad said it was my job to look after my little sister. But she didn't want any looking after. She never followed me around. I followed *her* around."

"Did you play games together?"

"Why are you asking me all these questions? You're not planning to write something about her, are you?"

"No, not at all." (Was that true?) "It's just that I was too— scared, I suppose—to ask her stuff like that when she was alive. And I never even knew she had a brother. I guess I'm trying to catch up on knowing her. Even though it's obviously too late in one sense."

"Join the club," he replied, raising his glass to me.

"You have how many children?" (Why was I asking this? I was hardly going to write a biography of *him*.)

"Two. One of each. And she was a good auntie. In her own particular way."

"Of course. How else?"

"She never forgot their birthdays. Or Christmas. If I sent them up to town she'd always be at the barrier waiting for them. They knew they could trust her absolutely. They'd go to a museum or gallery, but she'd always make it fun for them. Not 'This is a great painting by a great master,' but she'd stand them in front of it and after a while say something like, 'Can you spot the squirrel in the background?' Then there'd be lunch. And she'd buy them ice cream and chocolate and so on. Of course, she didn't exactly take them to the funfair, if you know what I mean."

Elizabeth Finch on the dodgems—now that would be a sight.

But his mood had suddenly shifted.

"She said a funny thing to me when she was in hospital. Strange, I mean, not funny. It was awful to see her, all thin and bony. Not that she had much flesh on her at the best of times. Though I must say she managed to make a hospital gown look elegant. I was pretty wound up, as you might imagine. But I knew she wouldn't have wanted me to break down, or tell her all the things I'd never told her before. So all I said was, 'It's a bastard, cancer, it's such a fucking bastard, Liz, a fucking bastard.'

"She turned her head towards me, and I saw those eyes of hers—you remember how big they were—and now they looked huge in this shrunken, skull-like head. She smiled faintly and whispered, 'Cancer, my dear Christopher, is morally neutral.' What do you think she meant by that?"

I paused. I was taken back to her teaching. I could have mentioned railways and monoculture, but I didn't think this would have been any help. So instead I just said, "I think she was agreeing with you. In her own way."

He didn't ask me to explain, just smiled and said, "That's nice."

We both sat in silence for a while. I ordered another bottle of wine.

"Did you . . . can I ask you . . . did she ever talk about her private life?"

"What do you think?"

"I think she didn't."

"She could have been married for all I knew. Several times. To a succession of Buddhist monks." There was a posthumous irritation—even resentment—in his voice.

"You never saw her with a man?"

"No, never. Actually, yes, once, by chance. We were meeting somewhere, not a station, but some kind of public concourse, and I was early. I suddenly saw her, about fifteen yards away. She was saying goodbye to a bloke. Tall, double-breasted overcoat, that's all I noticed. Because I was looking at her. She had put her hands out, flat in front of her, palms down, and he took them in his. Or rather, he put his hands underneath hers, palm to palm, so that she could press down. Then, when she had this support, she raised herself on one leg. I thought they were going to kiss, but they didn't. It was like she was climbing up to look at his face more closely. And her other leg, the one she wasn't standing on, she sort of stuck out backwards, at a right angle. It looked . . . peculiar, like a stork or something. Flamingo." He seemed embarrassed by the memory, even at this distance of time. His cheeks were normally pink—the pink of a countryman, or at least someone who sits long hours in a pub garden—but were they pinker now? It didn't matter: his unease was clear—as clear as if he'd caught her in bed with her overcoated companion. "Then she lowered herself back on both heels, took her hands from on top of his, and watched him walk away."

"Did she spot you looking?"

"No, and I knew I wasn't meant to do or say or see anything. I mean, that was obvious from all our previous life. But something got into me. I don't know how to describe it—righteous indignation, something like that. I walked up, kissed her on both cheeks—but formally, as we always did—and said, 'So who's your feller?' She looked straight back at me, as only Liz could, and said, 'Oh that? That was *nobody*.' Case closed, witness dismissed."

I could well imagine it. "And at the time she would have been . . . ?"

"Early forties."

When she was alive, I would have thought: that's Elizabeth Finch for you—what more did you expect! Now that she was dead, I could see how painful the moment must have been for Chris. A door might have been opened, but then his sister slammed it in his face, as if to say: back to your hutch, and your conventional life.

And the strange thing was that later, whenever I imagined, or reimagined, the scene, I found that *I* was embarrassed, as if I'd been there on that public concourse. And Chris's description somehow turned into one of my own memories. And I reacted to it as Chris had done—feeling that EF didn't have the right to behave as dismissively towards me as she had.

From EF's notebooks:

—I asked my GP if, when the time came, and the patient was beyond hope and unable to bear the pain, he or someone else would euthanise me. I added that I was clearly of sound mind when making this future request. He sympathised, but regretted that such an action was not permitted. I replied that, either way, I was hardly going to sue him, was I?

—The stylisation of the funerary address or newspaper obituary. The virtues have their boxes ticked. This is overt. But it depends on the less visible stylisation of memory.

—And then there is the inevitable third stylisation—of posthumous memory. Leading to the moment when the last living person to remember you has their very last thought about you. There ought to be a name for that final event, which marks your final extinction.

—None of the above should be mistaken for self-pity.

—I do not make the mistake of thinking that before the Expulsions and Persecutions of religious or ethnic groups there was social harmony. Evidently not: the very aim of an Expulsion was to make the state more peaceful. Get rid of the Troublemakers, even if it is we who visit Trouble upon them. Make the state monoracial and monotheistic, and all shall be for the best in this best of all possible worlds. Naturally, the plan never worked out, for two reasons. One, the animosity continued, so that instead of persecuting The Other within your own borders, you went abroad to persecute him within his. And secondly, reducing the diversity between people didn't result in harmony within. The narcissism of small differences ensured this.

Needless to say, her files contained no love letters. I imagine her reading them until she had fully absorbed all they had to say, and then throwing them away. Or perhaps she threw them away en masse. Obviously, I can't know. But she had a wonderful memory and a great dislike of clutter, so this is my conclusion. And naturally her definition of clutter would have been broader than most people's.

I used to send her postcards from my occasional travels. She never mentioned receiving them, and clearly kept none of them. One year I was in a provincial French museum and bought a card of a Bernard Palissy dish. You may know his stuff. He was sixteenth century, I think, and made fantastical pottery, highly coloured, often with *trompe l'oeil* fruit and salad leaves baked into the platter, perhaps with a lizard crawling over it. I imagine they were table decorations rather than actual serving dishes: talking points, as some would say. I've always found them great fun. Anyway, at my next lunch with EF, and against my better judgement, I asked if she'd received my Bernard Palissy postcard. Her answer was I suppose what I deserved: "There's far too much of him around."

Of course, I never sent her another postcard. And I'm also aware that I'm making her sound severe. She wasn't. Yes, she was. But she would have given that verdict with a light, ironic cadence to her voice. "Against my better judgement": yes, I should have thought about it before posting my card from Aurillac. Also: "great fun." Elizabeth Finch did "rigorous fun," as she had told us, but didn't do "great fun" any more than she did sentimentality. If, or rather when, her niece and nephew sent thank-you notes after their trips to London, as I'm sure they did, I imagine their words would have been carefully read, but not survive the day. I imagine Christmas and birthday cards might have had an even shorter lifespan. Perhaps EF believed herself above (or beyond) sentimentality. No, that's unfair, as it implies she might once have pondered the matter. She probably hadn't. She lived, and felt, and thought, and loved (here I'm guessing) in her own way, and at her own level. And it was also about clutter. Most of us hold on to our emotional lives tenaciously, revelling in detail whether good or bad, glory or humiliation. EF knew that these lives also contain clutter, which needs to be expunged so that you can again see, and feel, more clearly. Again, I'm only guessing.

Christopher and I became friends. Is that the right word? He would come up to town every six to eight weeks—"teeth collapsing again," "present for the wife," "see a man about a dog"—and we would have lunch. From my point of view, he was my link to EF; from his, I was, I suppose, someone new in his life who was easy to get on with. And I always paid the bill. He protested, of course, but I said it was only fair, given all the lunches his sister had bought me. But friends—when does that word start applying?

At one point, Christopher asked me—sounding not hostile, but mildly suspicious—what I was up to.

"Up to?"

"Yes, still asking me questions about Liz."

It seemed our obvious point of contact. But it was more than that. "As I said, I don't want to let her go. And I don't want her to congeal in my memory to a settled run of anecdotes."

He grunted quietly. "And are you planning to"—here he did air quotes—"'write her biography'?"

"I'm honestly not sure. There were so many gaps and no-go areas when she was alive."

"Too right."

"And I expect she would have hated the idea. Having someone 'crawling all over your life,' as an American writer once put it."

"Who was that?"

"John Updike."

Christopher shook his head to indicate benign ignorance. "And did someone write his biography?"

"Oh yes. Pretty soon after his death. Five years or so."

"Well, there's your answer," he said firmly. He looked directly, pale blue eyes out of a pink face. I couldn't tell whether he was approving or disapproving.

"You mean . . . ?"

"She's dead, you're alive, it's your call."

He made it sound obvious, even brutal. Later, I wondered about such certainty. In their lifetimes Elizabeth, though younger, had always been the senior sibling. Had death now reversed the hierarchy? Could it be as simple as that?

I've often puzzled over the relationship between men and women. (Men and men to a lesser degree, women and women hardly at all: the latter pairing seems obvious and sensible, not just as a matter of taste, but of necessity, given how the world has been fucked up by men.) Men and women: the misunderstandings and the misreadings, the false or lazy agreements, the well-meant lying, the hurtful clarity, the unprovoked outburst, the reliable geniality which conceals emotional indolence. And so on. The expectation that we can understand another's heart when we can scarcely understand our own. For myself, I have had two divorces and three children by different women. But does this mean I understand things better, or worse? It certainly means I am reluctant to give advice. But then, as I said, very few people come to me for advice, so I am rarely tested.

I knew a man once, seemingly happy in his life and marriage, a good father, secure in his profession, who always showed a generous and laughing face to the world. He started an affair—whether it was his first or not I cannot know—with, well, the sort of woman that sort of man might start an affair with. Ten years younger than his wife, but not dissimilar in social class and bright outgoingness. Maybe she drank and smoked a bit more than his wife—and who knows about the sex?—but she didn't have children. She was approaching forty, he was approaching fifty. There were the usual matters to discuss: what to do about the children (late teenagers, both problematic)? He was by nature clear-minded, but this was fresh territory for him, and so he vacillated. Yes, he would tell his wife, definitely, this weekend, promise; yes he would leave her, definitely, this weekend, promise; she must be patient, all this was new to him, yes of course he loved her. Several such deadlines came and went. Finally, he decided to be decisive. Yes, definitely, this weekend, cross my heart and hope to die; he'd tell his wife, and come to her on the Sunday evening. So, over the Friday and Saturday and most of Sunday, he broke the news to his wife and children: both the affair and his departure, and how he had so far imagined the future. Then he packed two suitcases, called a minicab, and arrived on the doorstep of his lover. Who did not even take the chain off the door, and through the crack told him to go straight back to his wife.

That's all I know. I heard it at second hand, and maybe retellings have over-rounded it into a story. I cannot quantify the damage, or trace any path of forgiveness, or think myself further into the participants' hearts. Of course, it is in some ways a banal story, but it was not banal to them as it happened.

I live alone, and have done for some years. You probably guessed. Though, as I may have said, this is not my story.

★

From EF's notebooks:

—"The world is poorly ordered, because God created it by himself. He should have consulted a few friends—one on the first day, another on the fifth, another on the seventh, and the world would have been perfect." AC.

Her notebooks contained some fully composed arguments, pertinent quotations, private jottings, memories, and mere scribbles. "Brown Eggs" is one such item, which might be the title of a poem by Elizabeth Bishop, or the first entry of an unfinished shopping list. Textually, it was what EF might have called an *olla podrida*, a phrase which would have had some of us scurrying to the dictionary afterwards.

I found this in Notebook Seven, divided into two neat columns:

Voltaire	Montaigne
Gibbon	Hans Sachs
Cavafy	Thom Gunn
Ibsen	Schiller
Samuel Johnson	Lorenzo de' Medici
Anatole France	Swinburne
E. Waugh? G. Vidal? Hitler?	

I looked at it for a while, and remembered how in her first address to us EF had said she would be giving us an optional reading list. If this had been it, I think I would have felt a little disheartened.

Here are some more personal entries:

—My mother, dying, told me that she would soon be looking down at me, and waiting for the day I joined her. She did not express anticipation of rediscovering her husband in whatever form she might find him. I smiled and patted her arm, which was the best I could manage in the circumstances. And since her death I have never felt either her actual or her theoretical eye upon me, not even in moments some, and certainly she, would consider embarrassing or shameful. She is mere ash, and my father older ash. I have always known this.

And:

—When I was young, there were "maiden aunts" around, who, by their very name, were held to be innocent of all to do with the body, transporting their virginity safely to the grave. Spinsters, a word now fallen into desuetude. The unmarried daughter keeping house for the widowed parent. Two sisters living together year after year, each fearing that some man would take the other, and each perhaps hoping that some man would come for them. (Chekhov.) Their separateness gave them social status of a kind, even if coloured by pity as much as admiration. I belong to neither of these categories. I have no desire for a sister with whom to share my life, and I declined (without being asked, it's true) to support my widowed mother except from a distance, and with money. As for the life of the heart, speculate as you will, but pity would not be appropriate; indeed, it would be insulting. Not that I can do anything to prevent it. But such is not my concern.

—"For a woman, fidelity is a virtue; for a man, it's hard work." AC. Ah, the facetiousness of the male epigram. To which I would reply:

—For a woman, love has historically been a matter of possession followed by sacrifice: that's to say, of being possessed and then of being sacrificed. And still it goes on, around the world. Better disguised, better "rewarded," but always there. My generation was in revolt against this (not the first revolt, by any means). We looked at our mothers, aunts, grandmothers, and saw women defined—also self-defined—at the point of their marriage (or non-marriage). A few had boldly resisted this, but most submitted for the rest of their lives. And for all my principles, I recognise that I am not immune.

And here are two jottings, clearly made at separate times, both in pencil, one darker than the other:

—M: Whither?

and then, beneath it:

—M: Why?

Somehow this—even if it was only two initials, two words and two question marks—sounded exactly like EF's voice to me. But if you ask the next two questions—M: When? and M: Who?—then I cannot answer.

I realise I am making her sound like a "woman of mystery." She wasn't: she had no "mysteriousness" about her. She was always exceptionally lucid. What she told you was always true, and made the truer by her exact choice of words. But when she didn't want to tell you something, she made it clear that she didn't and wouldn't. There was no middle ground, no sly hint or convenient evasion. "Oh, that? That was *nobody*." Nothing mysterious there. It was a lie, but she said it knowing that you would understand, and therefore it would become a truth.

When we had our student fantasies about her, they always tended to the louche or the glamorous. Why did we never have the opposite kind of dreaming: fantasies about austerity, discipline and withdrawal from the world? I can easily imagine her as the abbess in charge of a medieval convent: ivy-clad stone walls, silence, obedience, prayer and sacrifice . . . But no, such a speculation immediately collapses. EF was no abbess, and no St. Ursula, let alone one of her eleven, or eleven thousand, virgins.

Her notebooks show no principle of organisation. They range from intimate to formal; from personal reflections to lecture notes. Here, for example, are a few successive entries:

—Artifice, rigour, truth. Artifice in civilisations as much as in clothes. Artifice not the opposite of truth but often its very embodiment, what makes it irresistible.

—Pity as a form of aggression. *Beware of Pity* indeed.

—Of course, my kind of woman is out of fashion. Not that I have ever sought fashionability, or indeed ever had it. Sustainability is more what I sought.

—Oh, they say, she never married. Such a reductive way to describe and contain a life.

—I have quite as many friends as I need. They do not, on the whole, interconnect. Which makes some of them imagine that they are more central to my life than they are. Others, the opposite.

—It always used to be the case that when a relationship broke down, it was the woman's fault. If the man ran off, the woman didn't have the skills to keep him; if the woman ran off, she was flighty, or incapable of compromise, or lacking in stamina. Whereas in fact she was probably bored out of her skull.

—The student who told me, in all seriousness, that she did not like *Madame Bovary* "because Emma was a bad mother." Ye gods.

—And do not make the mistake of thinking me a lonely woman. I am solitary, and that is quite a different matter. To be solitary is a strength; to be lonely a weakness. And the cure for loneliness is solitude, as the wise MM once pointed out.

—People say, and I know so without hearing it: "Oh, things didn't work out for her. I wonder why. Perhaps she was too unbending, too uncompromising." What do they know? And what, I often wonder, does this famous "working out" consist of? A shared life of unspoken thoughts and cowardly conciliations, when part of you wants to take a breadknife to his throat as he snores complacently beside you.

—"Thou hast conquered, O pale Galilean." The moment when history went wrong. Romans *inclusive* of local gods. Monotheism v Plurality. Their connection to the life of the heart. Monotheism/Monogamy. "But love grows bitter with treason." Love dooms its adherents to "approximate happiness." Monotheisms always impose sexual orthodoxy.

And then I read the next entry, and knew immediately what I had to do:

—They say things are determined by genetics, by parenting, by heredity, by climate, by diet, by geography, by time spent in the womb, by nature, by nurture. They fail to hear the elephant in the room, trumpeting away: history. And if they do, they think history is what happened in their own or their parents' lifetimes: an invasion, a genocide, a plague of locusts. And that any history further back is inert, and has no chemical reaction with the present. Instead of looking at Hitler and Stalin, I suggest we look at Constantine and Theodosius. And if you want someone to admire, try Julian. What the newspapers would call "a hold-out hero."

And there he was, suddenly before me. "J, dead at thirty-one." Julian the Apostate, the last pagan emperor of Rome, killed in the Persian desert, conquered by the pale Galilean. I picked up the notebook with the reading list and went back to the boxes of books in the hallway. Swinburne, of course. Anatole France, an essay on Julian. Volume Five of Ibsen's *Collected Works*, entirely devoted to a 480-page play (how did they perform that? If they ever did?) called *Emperor and Galilean*. I looked up the index to *Hitler's Table Talk*, and there he was again.

I had let her down, distracted by my piffling divorce problems. I had apologised, and she had replied, "I'm sure it is only temporary," words which I had solipsistically misinterpreted. And she had done two things. She had left me a reading list in her notebook, and she had given me her library, rather—no, *exactly*—as the empress whose name currently escaped me had done with Julian, when he set off to campaign in Gaul. These seemed like the clearest of signals. Not some spooky "posthumous message," just a matter of me remembering and getting things straight and working them out. This was one task the King of Unfinished Projects was determined to complete.

To please the dead. Naturally, we honour the dead, but in honouring them, we somehow make them even more dead. But to please the dead, this brings them to life again. Does that make sense? It was right that I wanted to please EF, and right that I would keep my promise. And so I did. And this is what I wrote.

TWO

Those two initials in a notebook, with a page of blank space beneath: PG. I gave them slight, indeed whimsical attention. And then slowly realised that they stood for "Pale Galilean." As in "Thou hast conquered, O pale Galilean," in the poem "Hymn to Proserpine" by Swinburne. To recapitulate:

The speaker is Julian the Apostate.

The person he is addressing is Jesus Christ.

The location is the Persian desert.

The year is AD 363.

The words are an admission by Julian that Christianity has triumphed over paganism, Hellenism, Judaism, and all other competing sects and heresies swirling around the Roman Empire. Which for all time, now and hereafter, will be the Christian Empire as well.

As he utters the phrase, Julian throws a handful of his own blood into the air, and dies on the battlefield. He is acknowledging defeat of both a theological and a military nature.

The emperor's full name was Flavius Claudius Julianus, but since the victor acquires the spoils, and these spoils include not just the narrative and the history but also the nomenclature, he will be known thereafter as Julian the Apostate.

Of course, only some of this is true. Versions differ, almost from the beginning. The Roman army, after an unsuccessful campaign against King Shapur II, was retreating northwards through western Assyria, roughly parallel to the River Tigris, being pursued and harried by the Persians. The Romans (who in this case were mainly Gauls, but also Syrians and Scythians) were exhausted, hungry and far from home. The Persians had elephants, whose wondrous size and mysterious movement—as Hannibal had found out before—terrified the average legionary. A heavy skirmish took place. In the confusion, a cavalry spear is hurled at the emperor by an un-identified Persian; it grazes his arm and lodges in his liver. Julian may or may not have been carried to his tent on his shield. He may or may not have engaged his companions in philosophical dialogue as the life drained from him. He cer-tainly did not utter those famous last words which qualify him for an entry in the dictionary of quotations.

"Thou hast conquered, O Galilean." The phrase first occurs in Theodoret's *History of the Church*, written a century or so later. It is a brilliant invention—but then, historians can also be excellent novelists.

A millennium and a half later, Swinburne wrote, "Thou hast conquered, O pale Galilean." Where did that "pale" come from? Because throughout most of Western art, Jesus had been portrayed as having the skin of a northern European— Christ in whiteface—in contrast to the emperor Julian, who had been born in Constantinople and lived under a Middle Eastern sun for most of his life? Or is the Nazarene pale because he is otherworldly? Or because he is already dead?

More likely, though, the poet merely needed an extra syllable to make his line scan better. And so the invented line is reinvented, this time by a poet. Poets can also be excellent novelists.

★

It might seem strange that Julian "said" he had been conquered by a Galilean when there were no Christians fighting among the Persian army, and the officially recorded cause of death was a foreign spear. Ah, but was it? Early Christian mythologisers knew better: Julian had "said" the words because he had indeed been killed by a Christian hand and a Christian god. Two pairs of Christian hands, to be precise: a pincer movement between a pair of saints, Mercurius (c. AD 225–50) and Basil (fl. AD 370). One dead (in earthly terms anyway) and one living. St. Mercurius, the son of a Scythian officer in the Roman army, had been beheaded for refusing to take part in pagan sacrifices. But he remained active after his death and canonisation: he "lent his sword" to living Christians and future saints: for instance, to St. George (one of them, anyway) and, nearly a millennium later, to St. Demetrius during the First Crusade. In 363, Basil was praying before an icon which contained a portrait of Mercurius as a soldier with a spear. When he opened his eyes, Mercurius's image had vanished from the icon. When it returned, his spear was now tipped with blood, while, simultaneously, Julian was expiring in the Persian desert. How could a mere pagan resist such celestial firepower?

Julian was a Roman emperor who never set foot in Rome. He was an accidental emperor—though accidents led to imperial power more often in those days. He spent his early life as a scholar, far from court, far from military duty. In 351 his brother Gallus was summoned to court in Milan, made Caesar, sent out to govern the East, recalled after three years, prosecuted for corruption and executed. When Julian was in turn summoned to Milan, he was half-expecting to be eliminated too. But he found a protectress in the emperor Constantius's second wife, Eusebia, and perhaps the scholarly boy was not seen as much of a threat. He was put in charge of the empire's western army in Gaul and—by his own account anyway—expected to fail. Eusebia gave him books of philosophy, history and poetry, so that he could continue his studies while suppressing the various Germanic tribes. He crossed the Rhine three times in wars of pacification; his troops proclaimed him Augustus at the gates of Paris. He outwitted attempts to recall him to Milan, and marched to confront Constantius, who commanded the eastern half of the empire. As the armies approached one another, there was a happy accident: Constantius died of a fever at Mopsuestia in 361, leaving Julian unopposed.

By the Edict of Milan in 313, Constantine and his joint-emperor Licinius had decriminalised Christianity. The state thus became officially neutral in regard to religion, though Christian priests were granted free travel throughout the empire, and had no tax obligations. After Constantine's death in 337, his sons Constantine II and Constantius II then ruled as Christians. So when, on becoming emperor, Julian announced himself a pagan, and never again set foot in a Christian church, he was not disestablishing Christianity because it had never been established. The Christians of course, did not see it like this; and some suspected that if Julian returned successful from his Persian war, he would have turned his attention to the persecution of their Church. What was to stop him outlawing their religion again, and becoming a second Diocletian?

Julian had, in his personal life, many traits—austerity, modesty, chastity, scholarliness—which could equally be seen as Christian. In the "fleshpots of Syria," as they were always known, he remained untemptable; he was efficient, incorruptible, hardworking and fair-minded; he improved the judicial system, the tax system, and made the empire safer from invaders. But ... but ... but he was, and ever more would be so, an apostate. He was born and baptised a Christian, and grew up in the Church's observances, while still being permitted to philosophise Hellenistically. In his early twenties, he was initiated into the Eleusinian Mysteries, the ancient cult of Demeter. To its followers, it promised rebirth, advised chastity, and enforced total secrecy; to its antagonists, it was all dark caves, blazing torches, apparitions—the most pagan parts of paganism, a serious case of mumbo-jumbo. At the same time, for a decade, Julian continued acting publicly as if he were a Christian. Was this hypocrisy? Polytheism? Or merely prudence? Most of the troops he commanded in Gaul were Christians, who might be less eager to follow a pagan commander—and perhaps more eager to kill him.

All religions (well, almost all) hate the apostate much more than the ignorant misguided, idol-worshipping peasant who can usually, with a little stern persuasion, be hauled blinking to the light. Gibbon writes that the Jews at this time killed those who apostasised. Perhaps it's true of all large unitary organisations: Trotsky was assassinated in Mexico City for abandoning the one true political faith. But as well as hating apostates, such systems also need them: as negative exemplars, as warnings. Abandon the religion, preach against it, attack it, and see what you get: a spear in the liver, an ice pick in the skull. Had Julian been some dim and rollicking emperor, lustful and corrupt, cruel and duplicitous, he would have been easier to dismiss. But as one commentator put it, Julian was "at heart ... a Christian mystic gone wrong." Who said that thing about the narcissism of small differences? Yes, Freud. And so Julian became a bogeyman, a focal point of attack for many subsequent Christian writers, long after the religion was dominant throughout most of Europe and beyond. His reputation echoed on: Milton called him "the subtlest enemy of our faith." Later, Julian began to find support among Enlightenment thinkers, agnostics, libertarians and so on. Which helped keep his name and his fame alive. A figure to be interpreted according to the shifting light of history: for some, as EF ironically put it, a "hold-out hero"; for others, pretty much a younger brother of Satan.

Julian was a prolific writer, who dictated so fast that his tachygraphers were often unable to keep up. What has survived fills three volumes in the Loeb edition: Letters, Orations, Panegyrics, Satires, Epigrams and Fragments. A central text is "Against the Galileans," in which he lays out his objections to the Christian religion. It is a three-part work, whose second and third books have been lost. Even the first exists only in fragmentary form, often assembled from later Christian writers who quote Julian in order to refute him. But they hardly soften his opinions or his tone. The work begins:

> It is, I think, expedient to set forth to all mankind the reasons by which I was convinced that the fabrication of the Galileans is a fiction of men composed by wickedness. Though it has in it nothing divine, by making full use of that part of the soul which loves fable and is childish and foolish, it has induced men to believe that the monstrous tale is truth.

Julian deliberately refers to Christians as "Galileans" and Christ as "the Nazarene" to make their origins and beliefs sound more parochial. He sees the religion not as a development of Judaism but a perversion of it—so great a perversion that Judaism and Hellenism are closer to one another than either is to Christianity. Julian himself "reveres" the God of Abraham, Isaac and Jacob—who were Chaldeans; further, Abraham, like the Hellenes, believed in animal sacrifices, divination from shooting stars, and auguries from the flight of birds.

The foundation myth of the Galileans, the story of the Garden of Eden, is "wholly fabulous" according to Julian; also, entirely unfair to Adam and Eve, since God knew exactly what was going to happen—the divine thumb was on the scales. As for the Ten Commandments, they have "nothing unique about them," except for the laws concerning mono-theism and keeping the Sabbath. The idea of God being "jealous" is "a terrible libel upon God." Why would any rea-sonable person revere a punitive, control-freak deity who despises us and visits the sins of the fathers upon their chil-dren? Julian regards all this as juvenile and half-formed: "But all these are partial conceptions, and unworthy of divinity … the commandment Thou Shalt Not Worship Other Gods is calumniating divinity in a very high degree."

In defiance of their own Apostles, the Galileans have raised Jesus to the level of a god. They venerate the bones of martyrs, which is "peculiarly Christian and offensive to pagans." And look at some of the advice and instruction that they cling to. Jesus preached that they should sell all they have and give it to the poor. Imagine the practicalities of this, even for a moment:

> For if all men were to obey you, who would there be to buy?
> Can anyone praise this teaching when, if it be carried out, no
> city, no nation, not a single family, will hold together? For, if
> everything has been sold, how can any house or family be of

any value? Moreover, the fact that if everything in the city were being sold at once there would be no one to trade is obvious, without being mentioned.

Julian sets out what the Greeks and their fellow "barbarians" have given the world, compared to these upstarts from Judaea. "But God gave science, and the discipline of the philosophers, to originate with us." Astronomy began in Babylon, geometry in Egypt, the theory of numbers in Phoenicia. The Greeks combined and integrated all these disciplines. Does he need to cite names? "Plato, Socrates, Aristides, Cimon, Thales, Lycurgus, Agesilaus, Archidamus; or rather the race of philosophers, generals, artificers, legislators." The Hebrews haven't had a single general to compare with Alexander the Great or Julius Caesar; while Isocrates, son of Theodorus, is much "wiser" than Solomon.

The religions of the Greeks and the barbarians come out of long, deep, centuries-old civilisations. What, by contrast, do the Jews and the Christians have to offer?

But now it has come to pass that like leeches you have sucked the worst blood from that source and left the purer. Yet Jesus, who won over the least worthy of you, has been known by name for but little more than three hundred years; and during his lifetime he accomplished nothing worth hearing of, unless anyone thinks that to heal crooked and blind men and to exorcise those who were possessed by evil demons in the villages of Bethsaida and Bethany can be classed as a mighty achievement.

There is a lofty incredulity to Julian's attitude. How can a religion, based among the poorer castes of society, and without a true civilisation behind it, have come to conquer the Graeco-Roman world—declining as it was—in such a short time, and with such a deleterious effect? Especially when the laws of government, the form of tribunals, the economy and beauty pertaining to cities, the increase of disciplines and the exercise of the liberal arts, were only evident among the Hebrews in a miserable and primitive state? Part of the answer was just that: Judaeo-Christianity was not a civilisation with a religion, but an oppressive religion with little of a civilisation to back it up. Julian underestimated how this might be one of Christianity's unique selling points. "Civilisation" could come later, if at all; their religion *was* their civilisation. It was freestanding, therefore absolutist and—inevitably—monopolistic.

It was obvious to Julian that the adherents of such a religion shouldn't be allowed to teach Hellenistic philosophy. "If a man thinks one thing, and teaches another contrary to what he thinks, in what respect does this differ from the conduct of those mean-spirited, dishonest and abandoned traders, who generally affirm what they know to be false, in order to deceive and inveigle customers?" Further, those parvenu Galileans displayed a hysterical nature, as shown in their taste for martyrdom, which, as Julian puts it, "make[s] them think death desirable, that they may fly up to heaven, after having forcibly dislodged their souls."

Finally, the Apostate is baffled by Christianity's sheer lack of sophistication, its refusal to acknowledge experts, its preference for lauding the fool and the simpleton over the scribe and the wise man. Thomas Taylor, Julian's English translator of 1809 and himself a "philosophic polytheist," expatiated enthusiastically on this:

[Jesus] also seems chiefly delighted with little children, women, and fishermen; carefully recommended folly to his apostles, but cautioned them against wisdom; and drew them together by the example of little children, lilies, mustard seed, and sparrows, things senseless and inconsiderable, living only by the dictates of nature, and without either craft or care ... In scripture there is frequent mention of harts, hinds, and lambs, than which creature there is not anything more foolish, if we may believe that proverb of Aristotle, *sheepish manners*, which is taken from the foolishness of that creature, and is usually applied to dull-headed people, and lack-wits. And yet Christ himself professes to be the shepherd of his flock, and is himself delighted with the name of a Lamb!

It's worth pointing out that recent scientific studies have demonstrated that, contrary to age-old received opinion, sheep are in fact highly intelligent and emotionally complex animals, with good memories, the ability to form friendships and to feel sadness when their companions are sent to slaughter.

Publicly, Julian was opposed to violent measures. "I have resolved," he wrote, "to employ gentleness and humanity towards the Galileans; I forbid any recourse to violence ... It is by reason that one must convince and instruct men, not by blows, insults and torture." Further, "One should feel pity more than hatred for people so unfortunate as to be mistaken in matters so important."

This was principle, but also pragmatism. Miracles and martyrdom were the two great selling points of early Christianity. You died for your religion and gained eternal life: the notion still inspires some today. But Julian declined to persecute the Christians unto death. He obliged them to take the slow, winding, rocky path of terrestrial life. He made them sweat out the wearisome human span for a future chance of paradise instead of being propelled there directly in a turbocharged blast of their own blood. The tactic was cunning: deprive those eager to die of their martyrdoms and Galilean exceptionalism might not seem so exceptional: it might relapse into mere doctrinal dissent.

For the same reason, at the beginning of his reign, Julian showed "ingenious clemency" by recalling "the bishops exiled by Constantius. They were Arians, and he unloosed them on the Church." As the historian and soldier Ammianus Marcellinus put it: "For he knew that the Christians are worse than wild beasts when they dispute among themselves." Even more provocative was Julian's plan to rebuild the Temple at Jerusalem. Jesus had told his disciples that the Temple would not be rebuilt until his second coming—which would signify the glorious end of the world. The Apostate's cunning plan to give the lie to Christ's prophecy did not work out during his short reign; but such an approach was far more dangerous to the religion than the mere opposition of military might.

So Julian fell upon the Galileans with "gentleness," with mildness, with clemency, with a refusal to butcher—Christian virtues, you might think, all of them. But not Christian virtues which appealed to the Christians of the time, or later. Gregory of Nazianzus (c.329–90) was an early Church Father who had known Julian when they were both studying in Athens. In his writings he tries to portray Julian as a monster, while explicitly and consistently complaining how tyrannical the emperor had been in denying Christians the crown of martyrdom. A little later, St. Jerome (c.347–420) rails against Julian's *blanda persecutio*—persecution by methods of mildness.

Which reminds me of a joke from my schooldays. Q. What's the definition of a sadist? A. Someone who's kind to a masochist.

Ammianus describes Julian as follows:

> He was of middle height, his hair was smooth as if it had been combed, and he wore a bristly beard trimmed to a point. He had fine, flashing eyes, the sign of a lively intelligence, well-marked eyebrows, a straight nose, and a rather large mouth with a pendulous lower lip. His neck was thick and somewhat bent, his shoulders large and broad. From head to foot he was perfectly built, which made him strong and a good runner.

The beard is important: it is the sign of a philosopher; also— or therefore—of a man deliberately devoid of personal vanity. Julian made a point of not looking like a typical Caesar or emperor. When he was having distant, unexpected successes in Gaul, courtiers surrounding Constantius mocked him as "more of a goat than a man"; also, "a babbling mole," an "ape in purple" and a "Greek dilettante." When Julian himself inherited the court at Constantinople, he found it deeply corrupt, self-seeking and pleasure-loving, obsessed with fine clothes, fine fabrics and gluttony. "Triumphs in battle were replaced by triumphs at table," commented Ammianus. Soldiers had lost all discipline: "Their drinking-cups were heavier than their swords," their mattresses were of down, and "instead of their traditional chants the troops practised effeminate music-hall songs." Early on, seeking a trim, the emperor sent for a hairdresser. The man turned up splendidly dressed; Julian remarked, "I sent for a barber, not a treasury official." He asked the fellow how much he earned, and was appalled by the answer. He immediately dismissed "the whole category of these people, together with cooks and the like, who were in the habit of receiving about the same amount."

It was Roundhead versus Cavalier, Puritan versus papist. Hair both mattered and spoke. Early in his days as emperor, there had been riots in Alexandria, where the people turned on the Christian authorities. Among the lesser officials put to death were Dracontius, the superintendent of the mint, and his companion-in-crime-and-religion Diodorus. One of the latter's offences was that "while directing the building of a church [he] had taken the liberty of cropping the curls of some boys, because he thought that long hair was a feature of the worship of the heathen." The two Christians were roped together, killed, and their mutilated bodies loaded onto camels, and taken to the beach, where they were burnt and their ashes cast into the sea, "for fear that the remains might have been collected and have a church built over them."

On his way to Persia, Julian paused at the city of Antioch. It was offensive to him on many grounds: Christian, sybaritic, corrupt, tight-fisted and lazy. But it also contained one of the holiest pagan temples, that of Apollo in the suburb of Daphne, erected on the very spot where the fleeing Daphne had been transformed into a laurel tree. Inside was a statue of Apollo made from vine wood, thirteen metres high and wrapped in a gold cloak: it was said to be equal in magnificence to the statue of Zeus at Olympia. From Constantinople, Julian had sent ahead instructions to restore the temple and make it ready for his arrival. He had imagined beasts ready for sacrifice, libations, and the city's youth splendidly arrayed to greet him. But nothing at all had been done. When asked what the city of Antioch had prepared for sacrifice, the priest produced a single paltry goose, which he had brought himself from home.

But the problem was greater than indolence and insolence. The site had been polluted by Julian's own brother Gallus, who, when governor of Antioch, had built a church to St. Babylus, a local Christian martyr, right next to the temple, and transported the saint's body to lie there. At Delphi Julian had consulted the priestess of Apollo and asked why the oracle had gone silent. Her reply was: "The dead prevent me from uttering. I will say nothing until the grove is purified. Break open the graves, dig up the bones, move the dead." Obeying this instruction, Julian had Babylus's sarcophagus removed and returned to the martyrium from which Gallus had first extracted it. There were street protests verging on riot, and insults screamed at the emperor; a few Christians were arrested and "tortured with scourges and metal claws." A couple of days later, the Temple of Apollo burnt to the ground, incinerating all thirteen metres of the vine-wood deity. Naturally, the Christians were suspected (though a pagan worshipper careless with his wax tapers may have been the culprit).

The Antiocheans had given Julian a mixed reception (but then he had brought sixty thousand troops to billet on the city). They called him a monkey, a bearded dwarf, and nicknamed him Axeman for his animal sacrifices. Other rulers might have inflicted violence; Julian preferred to reply with a literary axe. He wrote and published a satire upon the city and its inhabitants, called *The Beard-Hater*. It is a strange and peripatetic text: part rebuke, part self-justification; matey in places, imperious in others; autobiographical and jesting, ironic and sarcastic; a theatrically self-deprecating mea culpa. It is as if Julian imagined that he could win over the population by humorous yet sophisticated complaint, plus a public examination of his own character. There is no evidence that it had this effect.

He explains how his nature and outlook on life have been formed: by the early death of his mother, by the eunuch who taught him, by his time spent in Gaul among the Celts. There is also heredity to consider: "The Mycians on the very banks of the Danube, from whom my own family is derived, [are] a stock wholly boorish, austere, awkward, without charm and abiding immovably by its decisions; all of which are proofs of terrible boorishness." As a result, he is indeed as they caricature him, if not more so: rough and unkempt, his famous beard full of "lice that scamper about in it as though it were a thicket for wild beasts." And there is worse:

> I seldom have my hair cut or my nails, while my fingers are nearly black from using a pen. And if you would like to learn something that is usually a secret, my breast is shaggy and covered with hair, like the breasts of lions who among wild beasts are monarchs like me, and I have never in my life made it smooth, so ill-conditioned and shabby am I, nor have I made any other part of my body smooth or soft.

He is a lice-ridden dwarf in a city of self-depilators: "All of you are handsome and tall and smooth-skinned and beardless; for old and young alike . . . rather than righteousness you prefer 'changes of raiment and warm baths and beds.'" He puts further insults into the mouths of the Antiocheans: the emperor is irritatingly temperate, falsely humble, affectedly over-pious. Whether readers of such ironic self-characterisation would be won over is doubtful. For a start, they had a direct point of comparison: Julian's brother Gallus, who had ruled as a Christian and built them a splendid new church. In a spirit of dark raillery, Julian refers to his uncle, the (Christian) emperor Constantius: "Bear with me, then, if I speak frankly. In one thing Constantius did harm you, in that when he had appointed me Caesar he did not put me to death." If this had been a public speech, the crowd would probably have applauded the line.

One of the problems of Julian's tract is that irony has its limitations. Being over-sophisticated in defence of his supposed boorishness does not convince—indeed, comes to seem irrelevant. Julian was never going to argue the Antiocheans into agreement, let alone submission: he was always starting from a losing position. At one point, in a pained manner, he asks, "What . . . is the reason for your antagonism and your hatred of me?" Yet the answers are plain, indeed woven into Julian's own text. The Antiocheans hate him because he has deposed their religion and reinstated paganism. He has blasphemously disinterred the bones of their local saint and martyr. He has interfered with their traditional ways of doing things. His attempt to stabilise the price of corn has backfired and produced stockpiling and inflated prices. He also sits in their courts and interferes with justice. More broadly, he shows contempt for their culture: he despises the theatre, is bored by horse races, scorns music and dancing. He advises them to discipline their women, whom, at the same time, he fails to be seduced by. He is an unsophisticated outsider, a stranger to civilised manners, an undepilated scruff—in short and in total: a Beard.

Towards the end of his complaint, Julian announces that "I willingly go away and leave your city to you." He realises that he has failed in Antioch, and so he departs, swearing never to return. He was an atypical emperor, reluctant to perform the traditional ceremony of slaughtering his next of kin and eliminating his political enemies, whimsically torturing and executing. As he was tolerant of other faiths, so he showed clemency to his foes after the battle was over— usually. But we must allow for the times, and remember an incident early in his military career when he was marching his troops from Auxerre to Troyes. Deep in the forest, they were ambushed by a force of Alemanni; outnumbered, and the fight seemingly lost, many of the legionaries were ready to flee. Julian's military career, and perhaps life, were at stake. His solution was to offer a personal bounty for each German head brought to him after the battle had been won. Thus encouraged, his troops were driven to a frenzy of killing, followed by the mutilation of their fallen enemies. Rarely has the word "headcount" held so much resonance.

When Julian set off for his eastern war, he took with him sixty thousand troops, the largest army any Caesar had led into Persia. He allowed his men large supplies of rough wine and biscuit. The emperor's taste for clemency was also less in evidence when on campaign. During the early part of their incursion, the inhabitants of towns without fortification fled at his approach; in Gibbon's words, "Their houses, filled with spoil and provisions, were occupied by the soldiers of Julian, who massacred, without remorse, and without punishment, some defenceless women." When they reached the fertile Assyrian plains, "the philosopher retaliated on a guiltless people [with] acts of rapine and cruelty." The taking of the city of Maogamalcha resulted in "an undistinguishing massacre"; while the governor, "who had yielded on a promise of mercy, was burnt alive." The city was razed to the ground, an action which left Gibbon coolly—indeed, snootily— indifferent: "These wanton ravages need not excite in our breasts any vehement emotions of pity or resentment. A simple, naked statue, finished by the hand of a Grecian artist, is of more genuine value, than all these rude and costly monuments of barbarian labour: and, if we are more deeply affected by the ruin of a palace than by the conflagration of a cottage, our humanity must have formed a very erroneous estimate of the miseries of human life." In other words: let's not waste sympathy on them.

Not that the ravagers were indifferent to what they found. After the surrender of Perisabor, Julian's soldiers discovered quantities of corn and arms, but also "splendid furniture [which was] partly distributed among the troops, and partly reserved for the public service." How much of this treasure made it back intact is not recorded. Doubtless very little, as shortly afterwards, when the Tigris had been crossed, Julian controversially—and literally—burnt his boats. His rationale was that, with the river in flood, it would be impossible to navigate upstream; while to abandon them unburnt made them a gift to the enemy. Also, Alexander the Great had once done the same thing.

While his soldiers pillaged and raped, Julian remained an aloof centre of temperance and sobriety. The theory of climate did not apply, even passingly, to him. Gibbon again: "In the warm climate of Assyria, which solicited a luxurious people to the gratification of every sensual desire, a youthful conqueror preserved his chastity pure and inviolate: nor was Julian ever tempted, even by motive of curiosity, to visit his female captives of exquisite beauty, who, instead of resisting his power, would have disputed with one another the honour of his embraces."

★

Julian is often described—and not just by his militant opponents—as a fanatic; even if a tolerant or clement one. The charge refers first to his deep involvement in the mystical side of his religion. (Non-pagans tend to prefer paganism with a calmer, more philosophical face to it.) Secondly, Julian was thought to go too far—far too far—in the matter of prognostication. His world was crammed with pagan gods, all of whom had their different competences and specialisms, which had to be acknowledged and revered. There were oracles to be consulted, and many birds and animals to be slaughtered and dissected.

As well as external signs and portents, there were also internal ones—from body and soul. Nor was this amateurish "There's a tingling in me bones" stuff; a proper philosophical theory lay behind it. "Coming events," writes Ammianus, "are also revealed by a burning sensation in men's hearts, which result in prophetic words." According to the natural philosophers, "Our minds are, as it were, sparks sent out by the sun, which is the mind of the universe, and that when they are kindled into flame they become aware of the future. Hence the Sibyls often say that their hearts burn within them and that a great flame is consuming them."

Then there are dreams to be interpreted. Ammianus quotes Aristotle as saying that dreams are "certain and reliable" when the dreamer is in a deep sleep "with the pupil of his eye looking straight before him and not directed to either side." You might have thought that with so many different prognosticatory tools at their disposal, augurers and emperors would come up with a surefire prediction, if only by a system of cross reference. But did the bird's guts agree with your dream, your burning heart, and what the sibyl in the cave said while wreathing her truths in doublespeak?

There was also a built-in catch to divination. As Cicero wrote: "The gods give us signs of future events. If we go wrong about them it is not the divinity but men's interpretation that is at fault." So we are continually reminded of their infallibility, and our own fumbling fallibility.

When marching from the pacified Western Empire towards a confrontation with his uncle Constantius, Julian halted in Dacia and "busied himself with the inspection of the entrails of sacrifices and with the observation of the flights of birds." The answers, not for the first time, were "ambiguous and obscure." Then a Gallic rhetorician, whose speciality was divination from entrails, discovered a liver covered with a double layer of skin, which apparently promised a successful campaign. Quite how and quite why, Ammianus does not tell us. But in any case there was a complication: Julian feared that this might be a false augury, designed to flatter him. So he dawdled on in Dacia until he received a convincing sign himself. And one day, as he was mounting his horse, the soldier whose right hand was supporting the emperor's foot slipped, and the man fell to the ground. You might fear for his skin; but Julian read this moment not as human incompetence, but an indication from the gods that "he who had raised Julian to high station" (i.e., Constantius) had himself fallen. Still, Julian havered, until envoys arrived to confirm that Constantius had indeed died at the moment the soldier had slipped, and on his deathbed had proclaimed Julian his successor. A miraculous coincidence, or just the normal reality with which the gods organised the world beneath them? Whichever, a sign for once had been correctly interpreted.

Nor, while preparing for his Persian campaign, did Julian hold back on divination. As Ammianus puts it, "The victims with whose blood he drenched the altars of the gods were all too numerous. On occasion he sacrificed a hundred bulls and countless flocks of other animals, as well as white birds, for which he combed land and sea." Fanaticism, or military professionalism? Either way, there was a comical by-product to these activities:

> The result was seen in the intemperate habits of the troops, who were gorged with meat and demoralised by a craving for drink, so that almost every day some of them were carried through the streets to their quarters on the shoulders of passers-by after debauches in the brothels.

After Julian crossed the Euphrates and marched into Assyria, halts for divination increased, and quarrels broke out between contenders for the emperor's ear. For instance, there was a band of Etruscan soothsayers, who had brought with them special manuals for use in time of war: these announced a prohibition on entering someone else's territory, even if the cause was rightful. This Etruscan warning was met with "contemptuous dismissal" by the group of philosophers, who were currently in the ascendant.

But what was a sign from the gods and what wasn't? On the evening of 7 April 363, there was an approaching cloud, which turned into an enveloping whirl of dust, which gave way to a full-blown storm in the course of which a certain Jovian and the two horses he was leading back from watering were struck dead by a thunderbolt. Experts in climate divination concluded that this phenomenon fell into the wonderfully named category of "an advisory thunderbolt." The campaign, by their interpretation, should not proceed. Once again, however, the philosophers rubbished this explanation, and declared

that it was a perfectly normal weather event, and if it por-
tended anything at all, it was just nature doing honour to the
emperor. The campaign proceeded.

After a successful engagement outside Ctesiphon, in
which 2,500 Persians were reportedly killed to seventy
Romans, Julian sacrificed to Mars the Avenger to ensure
continuing success. Ten fine bulls were ordered for this
purpose,

> but before they reached the altar nine of them sank to the
> ground by their own volition. The tenth, which broke its
> halter and escaped, was recovered with difficulty, and when
> it was slaughtered the omens it gave were unfavourable. At
> the sight of them Julian cried out in indignation.

And then what did he do? Punish the purveyor of fine bulls
for sacrifice? Or worse? Not at all. He "swore by Jupiter that
he would never sacrifice to Mars again." A testy overreac-
tion? A foolish tempting of fate? "Nor did he ever revoke his
vow, since afterwards he was carried off by death."

And that death was itself preceded by much material for
prognostication. The night before, "the shape of the genius of
the Roman people appeared to him" as it had done when he
was raised to the dignity of Augustus in Gaul; but this time
the vision departed "in sadness through the curtains of his
tent with its head and horn of plenty veiled." Then Julian
went outside and saw "a blazing light like a falling star" and
was "horror-struck by the thought that the star of Mars had
appeared to him in this manifestly threatening form." The
Etruscan diviners were summoned, and again announced
that battle should be deferred; the Etruscan diviners were
again dismissed. They begged him to at least put off his

departure for a few hours, but "although they brought to bear their entire knowledge of divination," they could not obtain any concession. Julian marched, Julian died.

"Have you heard? / It's in the stars / Next July we collide with Mars / Well, did you evah?"

For his supporters down the centuries, Julian was that seductive thing: a Lost Leader. What if he had ruled for another thirty years, marginalising Christianity year by year, and gently, then forcibly, recementing the polytheism of Greece and Rome? And what if the policy was pursued by his successors down the centuries? What then? Perhaps no need for a Renaissance, since the old Graeco-Roman ways would be intact, and the great scholarly libraries undestroyed. Perhaps no need for an Enlightenment, because much of it would already have happened. The age-long moral and social distortions imposed by a vastly powerful state religion would have been avoided. By the time the Age of Reason came around, we would already have been living in it for fourteen centuries. And those surviving Christian priests with their peculiar, eccentric but harmless beliefs—or rather, beliefs made harmless—would rub shoulders on equal terms with pagans and druids and spoon-benders and tree-worshippers and Jews and Muslims and so on and so on, all under the benign and tolerant protection of whatever European Hellenism developed into. Imagine the last fifteen centuries without religious wars, perhaps without religious or even racial intolerance. Imagine science unhindered by religion. Delete all those missionaries forcing belief on indigenous people while accompanying soldiers stole their gold. Imagine the intellectual victory of what most Hellenists believed—that if there was any joy to be had in life, it was in this brief sublunary passage of ours, not in some absurd Disney-fied heaven after we are dead.

Of course, such alternative history is just as much a fantasy as the Christian heaven. As Elizabeth Finch would have been the first to point out, we have to deal each day with the crooked timber of humanity. Unreason and greed and self-interest: can they be bred out of humanity? We also have to factor in fear as an influence on behaviour: fear of hellfire, of being cast out from God's grace, of an eternity of damnation. Even if enforced virtue can hardly count as true virtue. But it was an argument used against the Enlightenment thinkers: loosen the bonds of Christian instruction and command, delete the notion of a Final Judgement, and what is there to stop men and women turning feral? Not that any of those Enlightenment philosophers went feral. Ah, but what about the common people? Strange perhaps for a religion to so mis-trust its own congregation. The priest would reply, of course, that it is the shepherd who best knows his flock. But the Church had a watchfulness bordering on paranoia about los-ing its power and its hold. Which brings us back to Julian.

I wish I had been able to discuss all this with Elizabeth Finch. She would have modified my crude thought, and helped smooth out (or rough up) my narrative. Might I be doing what she might have hoped I would be doing? There are too many imponderables in that sentence for it to be meaningful. But it shows me how much I still miss her.

And as she might have pointed out, it could have ended quite differently. Rulers, with few exceptions, become more conservative and less tolerant as the years pass. So what if Julian, in those extra thirty or more years we grant him, had discovered that his policy of persecuting the Galileans with mildness wasn't working fast enough? Perhaps because his wily opponents kept finding ways to achieve multiple martyrdoms. There might have been more arson attacks on pagan temples, even attempts on the emperor's very life. What if he had then subjected Christians to *peine forte et dure*—crushing them beneath heavy stones—and reduced their religion to a state of frailty? He gave them the martyrdoms they claimed to seek—and then some. Whereupon he discovered a great fall in the numbers of Galileans on the planet: cruelty, it seemed, worked as well, if not better, than mildness. Then, for the few remaining members of this increasingly marginalised sect, Julian's name would send a shiver down the centuries, his name ever more worthy of anathema.

Instead, it was the Christians who came to write Julian's story. Theodoret of Cyrus (*c.*393–*c.*460) had two main points to make. Julian, supposedly a brilliant general, was in fact a poor strategist who made elementary mistakes: burning his boats left his troops downhearted, as did marching them across a parched desert in forty-degree heat. The emperor had failed to order enough supplies in advance, and also failed to loot the country he passed through with any efficiency.

Theodoret's second and wider point was about the nature of the pagan gods. Be they crafted in a German forest or a Greek temple, the fact was that they were just not very good at being gods. It wasn't that they didn't exist, rather, the many pagan gods were simply not as strong as the single (or tripartite) Christian one, plus all the accumulated saints and martyrs. Pagan gods were fickle and flakey: "Ares," wrote Theodoret, "who raises the din of war had never come to Julian as promised; Loxias had given lying divination; while the god who delights in throwing thunderbolts had failed to despatch one in the direction of the man who killed Julian."

It was a political as well as religious argument: not only is our religion truer, but our God is stronger and more reliable. You're better off with us. Vote Galilean!

Q. What happens (in the minds of men and women) when a god is no longer worshipped? Does he cease to exist? Or does he continue to circle the earth like another piece of space junk, beeping hopefully on a dead wavelength?

Compare and contrast the following belief systems:

A. We are all subject to the will of God, and to His power. God must be worshipped dutifully and often. God gives us signs and warnings, which we need to understand and interpret. This life is only the preparation for a further life, when the spirit is separated from the body. A man might find a way of hastening this separation.

B. We are all subject to the will of the gods, and to their powers. The gods must be worshipped dutifully and often. The gods give us signs and warnings, which we need to understand and interpret. The soul's bliss is of a higher order than the body's, so the separation of the better from the worse should cause us to rejoice rather than grieve. A man might find a way of hastening this separation. He might also know the place where he is destined to die, and the place where he will be buried, so that he may proceed towards them with calm assurance.

From the distance of time, differences appear smaller, even if the narcissism and paranoia arising from them remain great. One cause is the bossy nature of monotheism. "Thou shalt have one God only; who / Would be at the expense of two?" as Arthur Hugh Clough put it. And it *is* an expense to have merely one God, because He has all the answers, gives all the advice, requires all the worship. He does not subcontract, the Christian God; He is a jealous multitasker. Whereas the pagan and Hellenistic gods are multiple and multifarious. You have your favourite gods, each of whom is in charge of separate activities, and they have their favoured human beings. Of course they frequently quarrel among themselves, and humans are often collateral damage. They may abandon you on a whim: that is why you always need to curry favour with them. Splash out on another white bull! They keep you on your toes, these multiple gods. More than the Christian God? It's a tight call.

The second ineradicable difference between belief systems A and B is this: what happens afterwards. Both systems agree that there is the body, and within it the soul, and that at death the soul floats free and flies upwards—verticality being the preferred metaphor. And then? With Christianity, this is where the real drama of our existence begins. Life on earth has been a messy and merely preliminary matter: skulking in an outhouse waiting for the doors of the Big Mansion to open. After this paltry terrestrial span, there is life everlasting in paradise—or death everlasting in hell. The moment of judgement has come. And then there is a further matter— about matter. The most startling invention of the Galileans was the General Resurrection of the Body. Platonists found this not only absurd but disgusting—the notion that we shall be forever saddled with our bodies, down to the last corn, cataract and bunion.

In his eloquent dying words (almost certainly composed by Ammianus), Julian remarks that "the separation of the nobler substance should be the subject of joy, rather than of affliction." He offers his "tribute of gratitude to the Eternal Being, who has not suffered me to perish by the cruelty of a tyrant, by the secret dagger of conspiracy, or by the slow torture of lingering disease." Rather, the Eternal Being—which is not a god, but rather Julian's own personal daemon, entrusted with looking after him—has allowed him to die (or arranged, or instructed him to die) in full possession of his powers and "in the midst of an honourable career." His personal daemon, we can't help noticing, has allowed him to die only eighteen months into his project of restoring Hellenic paganism as the preferred religion of the Roman Empire—a project that will now expire with him in the Persian desert.

After Julian's self-eulogy, he instructed those around him not "to disgrace, with unmanly tears, the fate of a prince who in a few moments would be united with heaven, and with the stars." This union of the human soul with the divine ethereal substance is "the ancient doctrine of Pythagoras and Plato, but it seems to exclude any personal or conscious immortality," according to Gibbon. It takes a robust mind to contemplate extinction without wavering. On the other hand, it takes a robust mind to contemplate being judged by an omnipotent divine being.

Even if Julian did not pronounce those famous last words of his, the Christians had won, and they knew it. As proof, there was very little punishment or persecution of the Apostate's close companions and co-believers: they had been theologically disarmed. For the next millennium and a few centuries, Christians had control of the story and its message; and Julian remained a key figure in their anti-pantheon, worthy of mention in the same fetid breath as Herod, Pilate and Judas, his name a shorthand for evil, his striking-down proof of God's justice and His unflagging defence of His one true and monotheistic Church. "Monotheistic"—strange how, every time I type that word, I find myself thinking of EF.

But such parables rarely survive uncontaminated. Julian gets tangled up in tales of martyrdom in which he took no part. Later, he moves into quasi-secular contexts, in versions high and low. In 1498 Lorenzo de' Medici wrote a play in which Julian is less a medieval monster, more a Renaissance hero who comes to a tragic end. In 1556, Hans Sachs (he of *Die Meistersinger*) produced a ballad-play called *Julian the Emperor While Bathing*. Julian has been on a boar hunt; afterwards, while taking a swim, his clothes are stolen by an angel. Without such regal attire, the emperor becomes unrecognisable to his courtiers and even to his wife. He loses all power and value. Thus humbled, the pagan begs the Christian God's forgiveness, and—rather surprisingly, you might think—gets his clothes, his throne and his empire back.

The first modern, independent thinker to apply his judgement to the Apostate was Michel de Montaigne (1533–92) in his essay "On the Freedom of Conscience." The Frenchman was a Stoic, sceptic, Epicurean, and tolerant deist beneath a politic carapace of Catholicism. He grew up speaking Latin, and knew a little Greek (whereas Julian grew up speaking Greek, and knew a little Latin). Both men cultivated an indifference, verging on contempt, for death. And both found themselves at the centre of religious strife. Montaigne lived through most of the Wars of Religion, which maimed France between 1562 and 1598, leaving three million dead.

Montaigne begins his essay by considering "the present quarrel which is driving France to distraction with its civil wars." One of its causes, and fatal consequences, was that Reason had become overtaken by Passion. Even "men of reason" among the ruling Catholics whom Montaigne supported had been driven to actions which were "unjust, violent and rash." And it had been ever thus: Montaigne refers us to the early Christian period "when our religion began to be backed by the authority of law." Such power led to an excess of purifying rage, and the vast destruction of "pagan books, causing the learned public to suffer staggering losses. I reckon that this inordinate zeal caused more harm to literature than all the fires started by the barbarians." Christian zealots, for example, had attempted to exterminate every copy of the *Histories* of Tacitus (and nearly succeeded) all because of what Montaigne calls "five or six wretched sentences hostile to our religion."

Julian therefore offers a potent example from the ancient to the modern world. Even though he was "altogether vicious" in matters of religion, and "an enemy harsh towards us ... but not cruel," the Apostate was, for Montaigne, "a truly great and outstanding person." He left behind "examples of model behaviour in every single field of virtue: chastity, justice, sobriety, philosophy." He also "greatly excelled in all branches of literature." You can sense the strong appeal of one writer-philosopher for another. And Montaigne smilingly repeats the quip about Julian's overzealous paganism: "His contemporaries laughed at him ... [and] said that if he had managed to gain victories over the Parthians, his sacrifices would have exhausted the world's entire stock of bulls!"

In 1644, Milton made a speech to the English Parliament, later printed as *Areopagitica*, arguing against the official licensing—and therefore potential censorship—of printing. It is one of the great, passionate defences of free speech, which for Milton is key not just to the promotion of learning but also to the promotion of virtue. Further, it typifies the country which Parliament represents: "a nation not slow and dull, but of quick, ingenious and piercing spirit." Milton argues from both principle and practice. Censorship, he claims, is simply ineffective: it is like "the exploit of that gallant man who thought to pound up the crows by shutting his park gate." Milton insists: "Give me the liberty to know, to utter, and to argue freely, according to conscience, above all liberties."

This is not just a high-minded argument for the ages, but a political one of its time. For what was more alien to English Protestant libertarianism than Roman Catholicism: an oppressive papacy, a "tyrannous" Inquisition, the *Index*, censorship, the persecution of Galileo and many others. In its early days, of course, the Church was more persecuted than persecuting; and here Milton cites Julian the Apostate as "the subtlest enemy of our faith." You might think Julian a paradoxical choice in this context: after all, the massive destruction of manuscripts and libraries and the consequent loss of learning was inflicted by the early Christians on the heathens, not the other way round. Julian, as far as we know, did not order the destruction of a single Galilean text.

But this is why he was so subtle: he may not have censored or destroyed books, but he did censor readers. The emperor's most dangerous tactic was "forbidding Christians the study of heathen learning." This might at first seem a small loss—indeed, you might think exclusion from pagan books a welcome thing for a Christian. But the by-product of banning access to Hellenic philosophy and science, leaving the Galileans to teach only their own sacred books in their own churches, was to marginalise them and exclude them from civic rights and duties. Christians immediately saw the danger. As Milton put it: "So great an injury they then held it to be deprived of Hellenic learning, and thought it a persecution more undermining, and secretly decaying the Church, than the open cruelty of Decius and Diocletian." Happily, the Christian God spotted the danger represented by the Apostate, and acted through St. Basil and St. Mercurius. For Milton, "the providence of God [intervened] ... by taking away the illiterate law with the life of him that devised it."

The Apostate remained a vivid bogeyman for English Protestants, turning up again during the Exclusion Crisis of 1679–81. Charles II had ruled as a Protestant king since 1660; but his brother and heir, James, Duke of York, was a Catholic keen to restore the country to the one true faith. This alarmed many: the House of Commons voted repeatedly to deny James the throne, whereupon either the Lords overturned the bill, or Charles simply dissolved Parliament. Pamphlets and tracts blasted and counterblasted, the most famous by one Samuel Johnson—not the later Doctor, but the domestic chaplain to Lord Russell, leader of the Exclusionary cause. His tract had the extensive title *Julian the Apostate: being a Short Account of his Life; the sense of the Primitive Christians about his Succession; and their Behaviour towards him.* The giveaway word is "succession," while a subtitle explains the project further: *Together with a Comparison of Popery and Paganism.*

For Johnson, the Apostate was one of the great villains of Christendom's history: he is up there alongside "Herod the Persecutor," "Judas the Traitor" and "Pilate the Christ-Killer"; and placed "next to the Jews, thou hater of God." Happily, those Primitive Christians had "helped pray him to death," and he is now in hell, "undergoing excessive punishment." He was the great Hypocrite as well as the great Apostate; Christians called him not Julianus but Idolianus; also Bull-burner for his love of sacrifices. His soothsaying zeal was both revolting and blasphemous: for who should dare second-guess God over what is going to happen in His world? And while Julian himself might not have personally ordered the physical persecution of Christians, his predecessors, followers and associates had much blood on their hands. "At Ascalon, and at Gaza, where they rip'd up Christians, and then stuffing them with Barley, threw them to be devoured by the swine." While in the time of Constantine, a certain Cyril, Deacon of Heliopolis, "burning with a Divine Zeal," smashed up many of the pagans' idols. In retaliation, "The execrable Heathens . . . not only killed him, but cutting open his Belly, they tasted his Liver." Such impudent gastronomy was going a bit far, and was duly punished: as "the Historian records," shortly afterwards "their Teeth, and Tongues, and Eyes, drop't out of their Heads."

Lord Chief Justice Pemberton has declared that "Popery is *ten times worse* than all the Heathenish superstitions." Johnson continues: "Then I am sure we do no worse than the Primitive Christians, if we have ten times a greater aversion for a Popish successor, than they had for their Julian." It was a dismal prospect: "The Lives of all Protestants shall lie at the mercy of every Justice of the Peace, Constable, or Tything-man, who shall have Catholic zeal enough to destroy them. Every Commission-Officer, and Janizary, shall kill and slay without resistance." Papists would take English Protestants for "a fine glib and easy morsel."

Papists resemble pagans in three ways: being polytheistic, idolatrous and cruel. They worship "a vast number of false gods" and pray to saints of every kind—even saints for "Beasts and Cattel." They are bone-worshippers who pray to angels and the "omnipresent" Mary. Idolatry is the natural consequence of polytheism. "Christendom [has] been drowned in abominable Idolatry, of all the Vices most detested of God, and most damnable to Man, and that by the space of eight hundred years and more." Their male saints are like "Princes of Persia Land," their female ones like "nice and well-trimmed harlots." Papists have Pilgrimages, Candle-religion, ex-votos, stones that weep tears, miracle cures, and prostrate themselves before "any cross of Timber" or the slightest dried sample of Christ's supposed blood. They also worship a "contemptible" wafer, "a despicable patch of Bread, yes, though it have a crucifix printed upon it."

As for cruelty, papists exceed even pagans in this. "Nothing will satisfy them, unless they force their Idolatry upon us (as the French King sells his Salt), whether we have any occasion for it, or any mind to it or no." Many examples are given of the "blind Catholic zeal" now facing England. Johnson reminds the reader of the "Hellish plots" that had filled Elizabeth's reign. Those who would now welcome James as king seem to know "nothing of the Paris Wedding, the Gun-Powder plot, or the Irish massacre."

Johnson's tract earned him the nickname "Julian Johnson," and provoked others to join in: titles included "Jovian" and "Constantius the Apostate." It also brought him a heap of trouble, compounded by the execution of his patron, Lord Russell, in 1683, with a botched beheading by Jack Ketch on Lincoln's Inn Fields. Johnson himself was tried twice: first for seditious libel in 1683, when his book was burnt by the public hangman; and secondly in 1685, for unspecified "great misdemeanours." He was sentenced to stand four times in the pillory, to be fined two hundred marks, and be whipped "from Newgate to Tyburn." James II, now on the throne, was asked to intercede, but replied: "Since Mr. Johnson had the spirit of martyrdom, it was fit he should suffer." Johnson received 317 stripes "with a whip of nine cords knotted." He remained obdurate: while still under the surgeon's hands, he reprinted three thousand copies of his *Comparison between Popery and Paganism*, and published an account of his trial.

The high point of Julian's posthumous reputation came in the eighteenth century. Two aspects of his life and thought were particularly appealing: his famous—or notorious—"mildness," which translated into the Enlightenment idea of "toleration"; and his embodiment as a philosopher-prince, whose descendant was the enlightened monarch. Hence Diderot's relationship with Catherine II of Russia, who bought his library while leaving it in his possession and paying him to be her librarian. Meanwhile, Voltaire was much courted by Frederick the Great of Prussia: "My Socrates," sighed the king; "My Trajan," replied the philosopher.

First, though, there was Montesquieu. In his *De l'esprit des lois* (1748), he has high praise for the Stoics: "Indeed, if I could for a moment forget that I was a Christian, I would be forced to admit that the destruction of the sect of Zeno numbered among the great misfortunes of mankind." He goes on specifically to praise Julian as the finest of rulers: "After him, there was no prince more worthy of governing men." But he adds the rider, necessary for one writing at the time he was, that "This approval, thus torn from me, will not in any way make me complicit in his apostasy."

Voltaire established the modern interpretation of Julian in two typically combative entries in his *Philosophical Dictionary* (editions from 1764). From the start, he declines to use the "If I were not a Christian" caveat deemed prudent by Montesquieu. He even denies the emperor his habitual, derogatory subtitle of "the Apostate": there is no evidence, argues Voltaire, from either Julian's friends or enemies that he passed from a sincere belief in Christianity to a sincere belief in the gods of the empire; his "Christianity" was a necessary, life-saving cover—therefore he could not be an apostate. And now, finally, after fourteen centuries of calumny and invented nonsense from the Church Fathers and their successors, the age of sane analysis has arrived. The true Julian, far from the monster painted by his theological opponents, was "sober, chaste, fair-minded, brave and clement." And if, on the strength of facts, we must acknowledge that he didn't love Christianity, "we might find it excusable of him to hate a sect dripping with the blood of his own family." And though he was "persecuted, imprisoned, exiled and threatened with death" by the Galileans, he did not persecute them in return, and even pardoned six Christian soldiers who had conspired against his life. He had all the virtues of Trajan, of Cato, of Julius Caesar and Scipio, but without their faults. In sum, he was entirely the equal of Marcus Aurelius, "who was the first among men."

For Voltaire, tolerance and religious freedom were the two essential factors leading to enlightenment. Therefore, the two disasters of early Christian history were the imposition of monotheism and the fusing by Constantine of Church and State. Julian, philosopher-prince and paradigm of tolerance, far from being a brief historical aberration making a last gallant (or deluded) attempt to halt the advance of Christianity, can now stand revealed as a dazzling precursor to the Enlightenment. When writing to Frederick the Great, Voltaire paid the king the highest compliment in his lexicon, addressing him as "a new Julian."

Edward Gibbon, who had met Voltaire while studying at Lausanne in the winter of 1757–58, was to devote three chapters of his *Decline and Fall* to Julian. He rated him almost as highly as Voltaire did, though was made uneasy by the emperor's intense paganism. His final judgement was a little more cautious: Julian may not have had the genius of Julius Caesar, the consummate prudence of Augustus, the virtues of Trajan or the philosophy of Marcus Aurelius. However:

> After an interval of one hundred and twenty years from the death of Alexander Severus, the Romans beheld an Emperor who made no distinction between his duties and his pleasures; who laboured to relieve the distress, and revive the spirits, of his subjects; and who endeavoured always to connect authority with merit, and happiness with virtue. Even faction, and religious faction, was constrained to acknowledge the superiority of his genius, in peace as well as in war; and to confess, with a sigh, that the apostate Julian was a lover of his country, and that he deserved the empire of the world.

Gibbon admired Julian's steadfastness in the face of likely death: after the siege of Perisabor, he told his troops that "I am prepared to die, standing; and to despise a precarious life which, every hour, may depend on an accidental fever." But such high-mindedness ignored the practicalities of running an empire. Julian declined to nominate a successor on his deathbed, thus causing—in Gibbon's judgement—"the calamities of the Empire" by allowing Christianity to triumph. Very soon, paganism "sank irrecoverably into the dust" and "philosophers . . . thought it prudent to shave their beards."

What was left, apart from the example of his life, was his famous last stand against Christianity—the more famous because, for Gibbon, it was always doomed:

> The genius and power of Julian were unequal to the enterprise of restoring a religion which was destitute of theological principles, of moral precepts, and of ecclesiastical discipline; which rapidly hastened to decay and dissolution, and was not susceptible of any solid or consistent reformation.

Julian had dismissed the corrupt and venal court eunuchs when he came to power, just as he had dismissed the preposterous number of barbers. He might himself have given an example of austerity and simplicity, but that example wasn't followed by even those closest to him. As soon as he took possession of the palace at Constantinople, he summoned his old friend Maximus. "The journey of Maximus through the cities of Asia," Gibbon writes, "displayed the triumph of philosophic vanity"; and once arrived, "he was insensibly corrupted by the temptations of the court." After Julian's brief reign was over, Maximus became the subject of an official enquiry as to how "the disciple of Plato had accumulated, in the short duration of his favour, a very scandalous proportion of wealth." Before it had been eunuchs and hairdressers; now it was "philosophers and sophists," few of whom "were able to preserve their innocence or their reputation."

But there was a further, structural weakness to polytheism identified by Gibbon: it consisted of "a thousand loose and flexible parts," so that "the servant of the gods was at liberty to define the degree and measure of his religious faith." This might not have been a weakness, rather a tolerant strength, in other circumstances. Julian's approach to religion was certainly maximalist. His approval of Jews was that of "a polytheist who desired only to multiply the number of the gods."

Julian's own religious practices were intense, constant, and conducted at the highest level. According to the orator Libanius, the emperor believed that:

> He lived in a perpetual intercourse with the gods and goddesses; that they descended upon earth, to enjoy the conversation of their favourite hero; that they gently interrupted his slumbers, by touching his hand or his hair; and that he had acquired such an intimate knowledge that they warned him of every impending danger, and conducted him, by their infallible wisdom, in every action of his life; and that he had acquired such an intimate knowledge of his heavenly guests, as readily to distinguish the voice of Jupiter from that of Minerva, and the form of Apollo from the figure of Hercules.

Gibbon comments that such visions were just "the ordinary effects of abstinence and fanaticism" which "would almost degrade the emperor to the level of an Egyptian monk." Almost: being an Egyptian monk was a comparatively cheap business, whereas being on hair-ruffling terms with the top gods was ferociously expensive. Julian sacrificed every morning and night, and left nothing to chance, or to others:

> It was the business of the emperor to bring the wood, to blow the fire, to handle the knife, to slaughter the victim, and, thrusting his hand into the bowels of the expiring animals, to

draw forth the heart or liver, and to read, with the consummate skill of a haruspex, the imaginary signs of future events.

Top gods naturally deserved and got the top sacrifices: a constant supply of "the scarcest and most beautiful birds," transported from distant climes. Often, in a single day, a hundred oxen would be sacrificed. His troops, however, were approving of the emperor's assiduity, as they got to eat the leftovers.

Julian's name was common currency throughout the eighteenth and nineteenth centuries. Schiller spent ten years preparing to write a drama on the subject, and mentioned it to Goethe, but no trace of the project survives. The two men also formed an alliance aimed at stemming the decline of art and literature in Germany by publishing a series of journals (from 1789 onwards). But they had to supply much of the content themselves, and the result was not a great success. At one point, Goethe gloomily compared their task to Julian's unsuccessful attempt to roll back Christianity.

Byron begins *Don Juan* (1819–24) by sarcastically dedicating his epic to his fellow poet Robert Southey, who, like Wordsworth, had begun as a zealous revolutionary, only for time and age to weather him into a conservative member of the establishment. "Bob" Southey accepted the Poet Laureateship in 1813, which made him, to Byron's eye, "an epic renegade." The poem's dedication ends:

> Apostasy's so fashionable too.
> To keep *one* creed has grown a task quite Herculean.
> Is it not so, my Tory, ultra-Julian?

Theologians and historians adapted and rewrote Julian's life and thoughts to fit the purposes of the time (and of changing eternal verities). Few rewritings were as imaginative, or as personal, as that of Henrik Ibsen. *Emperor and Galilean* (1873), part of an early epic quartet of plays including *Brand* and *Peer Gynt*, was on a vast scale: "Why can't one write a drama in ten acts?" Ibsen asked rhetorically. "I can't find room enough in five." It was also, in his view, highly autobiographical. "I have put a great deal of my own spiritual life into this book," he wrote to his English friend and supporter Edmund Gosse. "I myself have lived through what I have portrayed in other forms; and the historical theme I have chosen has a closer connection with our own time than people might suppose before reading it." He called it "A World-Historical Drama," and also "my masterpiece."

It is certainly massive: 480 pages in the English-language *Collected Works* published in 1907. And when Ibsen refers to people "reading" it, he means just that; he calls it "a book" as much as a play. It was published in 1873 in an edition of four thousand copies, which quickly sold out; when the advance for the second edition came through, Ibsen invested it all in Swedish railway shares. This huge dramatic text is not in any normal sense a play: an interventionist director would have to quarry into it and discard much over-explanatory material to release the drama within.

Emperor and Galilean is seriously ahistorical; it drapes a thick cladding of nineteenth-century concerns over the known facts. These include: the need for human self-realisation; the fundamental importance of the will; and the incompatibility of Christianity with "the joy of life." There are familiar Ibsenite tropes like the pure woman (who might turn out to be not so pure) and the illegitimate child (whose existence would have come as a surprise to the real emperor's wife, Helena). Julian himself—like Ibsen, like Kierkegaard, but unlike the historical Apostate—is seen struggling to escape his deeply pietistic upbringing. He also belongs to Ibsen's line of idealistic but misguided reformers, convinced that he could alter the world's course with the help of a pure woman.

Early on in the play, Julian consults his mystical friend Maximus, who summons up the spirits of the three men who have most changed human history: Cain and Judas Iscariot appear, but the identity of the third remains shrouded—because, Maximus realises, it will be either Julian or Maximus himself. He also reveals that it will be the emperor's world-historical task to combine the wisdom of Christianity with the wisdom of paganism: a view much in circulation at the time.

Ibsen's Julian, far from being the clever, clement, non-violent ruler who preferred to outmanoeuvre his opponents, is presented as a full-on Roman tyrant. When he meets his death in the Persian desert, it is not at the hand of a mystery spearsman, still less by the miraculous combination of two Christian saints. Instead, he is murdered by the invented Agathon, a close friend who comes to the realisation that the emperor is the Antichrist. The dying Julian admits that his tyranny has been counterproductive; it has roused Christians most purposefully against him, and assured the future dominance of their religion. The law of unintended consequence has played out again, as it had for Cain and Judas Iscariot.

Emperor and Galilean had a great success as a book, but very little as a play. It took thirty years to reach the Norwegian stage—in 1903, three years before the playwright's death (and then only the first half was performed). Britain has always been loyal Ibsenite territory, but the play he called "my masterpiece" had its London premiere only in 2011. The (sympathetic) *Guardian* reviewer judged it "several degrees short of a masterpiece"; while the (unsympathetic) *Telegraph* critic called it "an almost unendurable bore."

A footnote, possibly of a pedantic kind. James Joyce's first published piece of journalism was an eight-thousand-word review of Ibsen's *When We Dead Awaken*. The *Fortnightly Review* paid him twelve guineas for it; Joyce was eighteen. He announced that Ibsen was the greatest thinker and psychologist of modern times: greater, specifically, than Rousseau, Emerson, Carlyle, Hardy, Turgenev or George Meredith. Unsurprisingly, the playwright was pleased by this assessment and sent friendly thanks to the young Dubliner. Nearly forty years later, Joyce paid him further homage in *Finnegans Wake*, which contains sixty and more puns on Ibsen's name and the titles of his plays. Thus: "for peers and gints, quaysirs and galleyliers, fresk letties from the say and stale headygabblers." The phrase "quaysirs and galleyliers" puns on *Kejser og Galilaeer*, the original title of *Emperor and Galilean*. Ibsen might have enjoyed this exhausting playfulness had he not been dead for thirty and more years.

And so we return to Swinburne, and his poem "Hymn to Proserpine," which I first heard on EF's lips all those years ago. In 1878 Swinburne wrote a second poem about Julian, "The Last Oracle," dealing with a much-repeated episode from early in Julian's reign. In 362, he despatched his friend Oribasius to Delphi to learn from the Pythia herself what his chances might be if he went ahead with the Persian campaign. Oribasius brings back not some gnomic message for diviners to ponder but the worst news of all: that the oracle is, in effect, permanently closed for business. The Pythia's reported words to Oribasius are:

> Tell the king, on earth has fallen the glorious dwelling,
>> And the watersprings that spake are quenched and dead.
> Not a cell is left the God, no roof, no cover
>> In his hand the prophet laurel flowers no more.

Oribasius duly reports these words to Julian:

> And the great king's high sad heart, thy true last lover,
>> Felt thine answer pierce and cleave it to the core.
>> And he bowed down his hopeless head
>>> In the drift of the wild world's tide.

Like "Hymn to Proserpine," "The Last Oracle" is a lament for the twilight of the old pagan gods and the unwanted arrival of the new religion—"the strange God's kingdom"—which has exchanged "Fire for light and hell for heaven and psalms for paeans." But the poet, while acknowledging the defeat of paganism by Christianity, also appeals over the heads of both religions to Apollo, from whom come all song and all sun, and who presides over everything: "God by God goes out, discrowned and disanointed / But the soul stands fast that gave them shape and speech." The poem's constant refrain and prayer is: "O father of all of us, Paian, Apollo / Destroyer and healer, hear!"

So Swinburne's two poems bookend the Apostate's reign: the Delphic Oracle falling silent at the start of it, and the emperor's dying cry at the end of it. In fact, neither "event" ever happened. Just as Julian's famous last words were a later invention, so Oribasius never made his pilgrimage to Delphi. It seems he only "remembered" that he had done so in old age, long after Julian's death. Furthermore, in 362 the Pythia was, in a recent biographer's words, "still active, if arthritic"; and she continued in precarious business for another two decades.

In Julian's time, the Western Empire was ruled from Milan, the Eastern from Constantinople. His favourite city was far from being a metropolis: Lutetia (now Paris) was just an island in the Seine, plus a few developments on the *rive gauche*—houses, a palace, an amphitheatre, baths, an aqueduct, and a Champ de Mars on which the Roman troops exercised. There was even the cautious cultivation of vines and fig trees. What Julian loved best were the severe and simple manners of the inhabitants. There was no falsity: in Lutetia, the theatre was either unknown or despised. The yet-to-be emperor "indignantly contrasted the effeminate Syrians with the brave and honest simplicity of the Gauls." Indeed, the only stain on the national character was "intemperance."

Gibbon allowed himself the pleasant fantasy of teleporting Julian into eighteenth-century Paris:

If Julian could now revisit the capital of France, he might converse with men of science and genius, capable of understanding and of instructing a disciple of the Greeks; he might excuse the lively and graceful follies of a nation whose martial spirit has never been enervated by the indulgence of luxury; and he must applaud the perfection of that inestimable art which softens and refines and embellishes the intercourse of social life.

Julian might also have enjoyed being feted by the French philosopher-historians of the day. But that applause didn't last. A century on, their successors had turned against him. The novelist Anatole France was dismayed and embarrassed by the treatment meted out to the emperor by Auguste Comte and Ernest Renan. "Comte is extremely hard on him," he noted. As for Renan, in his massive enquiries into the origins of Christianity, he is constantly, if passingly, disparaging. For Renan, Christianity was the highest expression of monotheism, and Julian's attempt to revive the old religion "an inconsequential caprice." Paganism was in a state of terminal decline, and the Apostate was simply on the wrong side of history. He stood in the dock with Antiochus, Herod and Diocletian, "all great princes of the world, whom popular judgement has consigned to eternal damnation." Out in society one evening, France heard Renan "mutter confidentially" to anyone who could overhear, "Julian! He's a reactionary."

France rates him much more highly: "Julian has afforded the world the unique spectacle of a tolerant fanatic." But he is also susceptible to a Romantic, indeed novelistic interpretation of the emperor as a young man who owed "his life and more" to "the Empress, the wise and beautiful Eusebia, who loved him." When he left for Gaul, she gave him "a whole vast library of poets and philosophers," so that, as Julian himself put it, "Gaul and Germany became for me a museum of Hellenic letters." France warms to a vision of the philosopher-prince on campaign, fighting the Huns while remembering the empress by reading her books.

And yet there is a paradox—at least to a sophisticated Frenchman:

> But of all men who have owed their fortune to love, Julian is perhaps he who took the least pains to please women. Eusebia must have had tastes somewhat unusual in her sex to have attached herself to such an austere young man. Julian, small and thickset, was not handsome, and he affected, by his deliberate negligence, to make his person more uncomely than it naturally was. He wore a goat's beard through which the comb never passed. It was his weakness to believe that a beard is philosophic when it is dirty.

Anatole France is as snooty as any Antiochean. Clearly, the emperor would not have cut it in a Parisian salon: he would have stood out like a Beat. As for being "small," he was five foot one, which Ammianus says made him "of middle height" for the time. France also baulks somewhat at Julian's combination of puritanism and mysticism. "A profound theologian and an austere moralist, he acted in accordance with the promptings of his conscience, and the impulses of a fate exalted by fasting and insomnia ... One shudders to think of an emperor who never sleeps."

Still, France does lead us to the overwhelming, if unanswerable question:

> Nevertheless, Hellenism, supple in its dogmas, ingenious in its philosophy, poetical in its traditions, would perhaps have coloured the human soul with sweet and varied hues, and what the modern world would have been like had it lived beneath the mantle of the kindly goddess and not in the shadow of the Cross is a great problem. Unhappily, this problem is insoluble.

By the twentieth century Julian's allure had somewhat faded. He was still well alive in scholarly circles; but elsewhere, he had shrunk to a historical figure to whom individual writers responded individually. That's how it seemed to me, anyway. And I must also admit that my zeal for research was diminishing. For instance, Nikos Kazantzakis wrote an untranslated play which ran for one performance in Paris in 1948: did I really want to pursue that? There was a baffling homage-poem by Thom Gunn and a dozen more lucid ones by Cavafy. But I quailed at Kleon Rangavis and Dmitri Merezhkovsky, and didn't get far into novels by Michel Butor and Gore Vidal. I seemed to be compiling a bibliography of the so-far-unread.

But the twentieth century did throw up one unexpected and unwelcome admirer of the Apostate. If Julian was a "fanatic," as some alleged, he had attracted the attention of the fanatic's fanatic: Hitler.

A quote from his *Table Talk* at midday on 21 October 1941:

> When one thinks of the opinions held about Christianity by our best minds a hundred, two hundred years ago, one is ashamed to realise how little we have since evolved. I didn't know that Julian the Apostate had passed judgement with such clear-sightedness on Christianity and Christians. You should read what he says on the subject.

I wonder if it's known who tipped the Führer off about Julian. In any case, he returned to the subject four days later, in the evening, when the special guests present were Reichsführer SS Himmler and SS General (Obergruppenführer) Heydrich:

The book that contains the reflections of the Emperor Julian should be circulated in millions. What wonderful intelligence, what discernment, all the wisdom of antiquity. It's extraordinary.

Also, previously, on the night of 11–12 July 1941:

The heaviest blow that ever struck humanity was the coming of Christianity. Bolshevism is Christianity's illegitimate child . . . In the ancient world, the relations between men and gods were founded on an instinctive respect. It was a world enlightened by the idea of tolerance. Christianity was the first creed in the world to exterminate its adversaries in the name of love. Its keynote is intolerance.

There is a thundering irony to this defence of tolerance. And at least Hitler didn't exterminate his enemies in the name of love. Unhypocritically, he exterminated them in the name of hatred and racial superiority. So while he might have admired the emperor, he certainly didn't understand him. As Julian wrote, "It is by reason that one must convince and instruct men, not by blows, insults and torture." As for the Galileans, "One should feel pity more than hatred for people so unfortunate as to be mistaken in matters so important."

THREE

Completing my essay on Julian both calmed and encouraged me. Of course, I showed it to nobody, because there was nobody to show it to except EF. It had interested me, and that was enough. It also proved that I was not the King—or rather, the Dunce—of Unfinished Projects. Now it was time to push on. If I had pleased her with my Julian (though how would I ever know?), it was time to continue honouring her.

Chris had asked me early on if I was writing a biography of his sister. I dithered in reply, because it seemed such a ... crude idea. The emperor Julian had brought me to the poet Cavafy, who wrote the following lines:

> From what I did and what I said
> Let them not seek to find who I was

Despite such discouragement, a biographer of Cavafy nevertheless emerged. The poet doubtless had secrets, doubtless sexual ones (who doesn't?) which he didn't want revealed. The poem ends:

> Later—in a more perfect society—
> someone else made like me
> will certainly emerge and act freely.

Even this poem remained unpublished for many years. But the instruction was clear: Leave me be, do not disturb these ashes. And Elizabeth Finch? I doubt she had the vanity to presume that anyone would "seek to find who she was."

Elizabeth Rachel Jane Finch, it said on her birth certificate; date, parents, registrar's name and signature. No marriage certificate, though that didn't rule out a Mexican wedding under an assumed name (chances of that: zero). Death certificate, yes. Will, yes: several small legacies, charitable donations, a direction that I receive her books and papers; then the rest to Christopher. If you google her, you will find a link to a newspaper website which gives a skewed account of The Shaming. I'm not sure how temperamentally suited I am to this task.

I asked Christopher about their parents. Their father had been in the fur trade; he was a man both devoted and highly anxious who could, just occasionally, convince himself that the comfortable suburban life he had won for his family might possibly last. He was correct in that fear: he died at the age of fifty-five from congestive heart disease. Their mother pretended it wasn't happening, or if so, it was some passing inconvenience, like gout. Elizabeth tended him on his way to death. She sat by him for hours, not talking, just waiting for him to open his eyes and smile; then she would smile back. It was all that was needed—as they both knew.

"And afterwards?"

"Afterwards, Mum stayed on in the house. She had her hair done every week, she supervised the cleaner and the gardener—though 'supervised' might be a bit of an exaggeration—went to the tea shop, played bridge, joined the local cancer fundraising group. Though I don't think fundraising was her forte either. And not that Dad had cancer, anyway."

"And Elizabeth?"

"She visited every six weeks or so. Purely out of duty. I

don't think there was any sympathy there. Or interest. On either side. Mother could be . . . self-absorbed. And Elizabeth could be . . . fastidious—is that the word?"

I laughed. I knew only too well.

"And she felt fastidious towards her mother. Not embarrassed, that wouldn't be true. But a sort of disbelief that her mother was her mother, if you see what I mean."

"A feeling you didn't share?"

"Well, I'm a simple fellow. I take the world as it comes, and try to judge as little as possible. And after all, a boy's mother is always his mother, not so?"

I didn't answer. In my case—but my case isn't relevant. I liked Christopher Finch, though doubted he could possibly be the simple fellow he declared himself to be. His sister couldn't have captured all the complications and subtleties available in their shared genes.

"And . . . how did it end?"

"Mum . . . It's funny about what charities you give to, isn't it? Like, I give to Dr. Barnardo's because I'm incredibly grateful I had a secure family upbringing. And I give to the lifeboatmen because I somehow think that will ward off me ever being in a shipwreck. Not that I exactly take a boat very often. Maybe a ferry occasionally . . . And not that I really believe in the superstitious approach to charity. So, anyway, Mum got cancer, how ironic, who'd have guessed? Liz carried on visiting her just as much, or just as little, as before. I took over. The doctors, nursing home, power of attorney, all that. Funeral. Lawyers."

"Can I ask what her will said? And your father's, for that matter?"

"Dad left everything to Mum. Mum left two-thirds to me, one-sixth to Liz, and one-sixth to various charities."

"And how did Elizabeth react to that?"

"With two words: 'Perfectly just.' Even though she knew Dad wouldn't have liked it. I offered to give her a share of mine, make it fifty-fifty, which is undoubtedly what Dad would have wanted; but she refused. 'Her wishes must be obeyed,' Liz said; and that was that. I was a bit relieved, to tell the truth, having a wife and two children."

"It was generous."

"Well, it was and it wasn't. I didn't, and don't, think she exactly did it for *me*. She did it because she thought it was the right thing to do. Anyway, Liz would have found the idea of challenging her mother's will . . ."

"Vulgar?" I was using the word in the narrow, Finchian sense of morally squalid—not that Chris would have known.

"Sort of. And anyway, we always got on, Liz and me. Even if it was entirely on her terms. From the moment she could speak, practically."

"And did you resent that?"

He thought about it. "I suppose I must have done, somewhere, maybe deep down. I was a normal kid, adolescent, so I must have done. But you see, she was Liz, and I was in awe of her from a very early age. And our parents never commented on or criticised her . . . assumption of . . . power. So I thought it was normal."

He seemed far away, back in his childhood, musing.

"Do you remember her showing an interest in early Church history?"

He came out of his reverie. "Now you've got to be pulling my leg there."

★

From EF's notebooks:

—Of course, they continue, she never had children, and even if she has "come to terms" with it, a childless woman is always, at some level, essentially unfulfilled isn't that the case? Such an interesting mixture of condescension and paranoia.

—I have nothing against children, you understand. I am a capable and loving aunt and godmother. It's just that they take so long to grow up. And they keep having birthdays. So many birthdays, and still no sign of adulthood. Such a design fault.

—A supermarket of religions, with the ultimate in consumer choice.

—Annually, on my birthday, I clear out my cupboards and shelves. It feels like an act of personal hygiene. And I sometimes wonder why those close to me imagine that I need so many scented candles, so much skin cream, so many jams made from improbable ingredients, so many tins of truffled this and truffled that, whose truffle content, when you look at the label, turns out to be approximately 0.05 percent.

And here she is working her way towards a lecture:

—Had churches been less monotheistic and oppressive, had the expulsions of those Not Like Us not taken place, Britons would have mixed more freely, miscegenation would have become normal, and whiteness no indicator of superiority. So a society with fewer evident markers of status and money and power. British history might therefore have become the story of a country learning from otherness rather than ignoring and repressing it. In place of a country of conquest, viewed from the outside with anything from wary respect to intense loathing, a country which led the world (or part of the world) differently—as an example of those virtues, often present in the society if frequently overshadowed, of tolerance, liberalism, and a good-humoured openness to others. Harder to achieve from our present position. So much self-propaganda to be unlearnt, so much getting our history wrong. Of course all this, if stated publicly, would attract the usual anathematising: defeatist, self-loathing, pinko, a watering-down of true English and British blood, enemies of the state, etc., etc. But DNA tests invariably surprise "white" people by showing a multiplicity of "origins." The folly of racial purity. In its place, an exaltation of what conservative fantasists would call "the mongrel state": yet this is not an ambition, rather an acknowledgement of what is there anyway and everywhere.

Over one of our Italian lunches, I once asked her what she did for Christmas, not knowing anything of her family, or its closeness of attachment.

"On Christmas Day," she replied, "I am a hospital visitor."

I was taken aback. "That's very . . . Christian of you."

"Charity is hardly confined to the Christian religion," she replied.

Later, I found myself wondering how she went down with some of the hospital inmates. How many of them wanted to discuss European literature? Did she wear a holly badge? But I was being facetious; also, not giving her enough credit. Some of them might have been delighted by this poised apparition; they might even sense, somehow, that she would not judge them. She might easily appear preferable to a soft and simpering hospital chaplain.

★

I said to Chris, after he'd had a few glasses of house white, "Look, this may seem a bit awkward . . ."

"Fire away."

"Your family was . . . Jewish, wasn't it?"

"Jewish?"

"Yes, something your sister said in class."

"What did she say?"

I gave him a rather doctored account of EF's exchange with Geoff.

"No, absolutely not." He seemed baffled rather than offended. "Why would you think that? I suppose Liz was dark and brainy . . ." We stared at one another, both equally surprised. But Chris, as I had discovered, rarely took offence, always preferring to turn life's opaqueness into a joke. "I mean, if you're asking me to drop my trousers . . ."

"Sorry, it was obviously just a massive mistake."

Later, I thought, But it wasn't a massive mistake. So it must have been a deliberate lie on EF's part. She'd said that thing about losing members of her family, and walked out. Into the silence, Geoff had said, "How was I to know she was Jewish?" I never doubted it, and later evidence only confirmed it: the furrier father who must have changed his name, the pampered, complaining mother (not that this wasn't a familiar trope in other cultures . . .).

But why? I came up with a small solution and a larger one. The small was this: EF thought that Geoff was grandstanding, and decided to take him down a peg. Hmmm. The larger one: she'd been pretending to be Jewish; or, to put it more strongly, she'd decided to pass as Jewish. Again, why? So as to confront English anti-Semitism when it arose? That didn't make much sense. Or perhaps: it was to do with arti-fice, with self-construction in some way. Again, why? Where was the advantage, if this were the case, in pretending to be a—non-practising, assimilated—Jew? Was it a style point, like her hair and her brogues? But EF was far too serious-minded for that, surely? Unless she'd taken the decision when she was younger and less serious-minded, and became stuck with it.

I decided to park the issue.

I sometimes wonder how biographers do it: make a life, a living life, a glowing life, a coherent life out of all that cir-cumstantial, contradictory and missing evidence. They must feel like Julian on campaign with his retinue of diviners. The Etruscans tell him this; the philosophers tell him that; the gods speak, the oracles are silent or obscure; the dreams alarm him this way, his visions propel him that way, the animals' viscera are ambivalent; the sky says this, the dust storm and the advisory thunderbolt insist otherwise. Where is the truth, where is the way forward?

Or maybe consistent narrative is a delusion, as is trying to reconcile conflicting judgements. Maybe you could equally account for someone by a mere list of snagging, indicative facts. For instance:

—When he sat as a judge in Antioch, the emperor fined himself ten gold pounds for having thoughtlessly infringed the authority of another magistrate.
—There is something Cromwellian about Julian: austere, puritanical, pitiless in combat. Consider this fragment, in which he complains about his overflattering depiction by a portraitist: "Why, my friend, did you give me a form other

than my own? Paint me exactly as you saw me." Warts and all.

—His success in reforming the tax system was based on his insight into both human nature and economics. Most citizens thought they were overtaxed, and so would hide their valuable possessions and under-declare their income. The traditional response of tax-collectors was to increase their demands to make up the shortfall. Julian, however, understood that if you lowered taxes, citizens were more likely to pay what was asked; they would be more honest, and judge the fiscal system fairer.

—After the storming and sack of Maogamalcha in AD 363, Julian declined his share of the spoils. He took for himself "only a dumb boy, who was adept at conveying with graceful gestures all that he knew of sign language, together with three gold pieces; this he considered a pleasant and acceptable reward for the victory he had won."

Does this advance things? Is it distillation or mere dispersal? Small incidents (and there could be a whole bookful) which come together, or merely an assembly of fragments? Or does it just provoke further questions—like, what became of the dumb boy after his master's death?

I was floundering; a desperation of doubt fell upon me. Then I remembered reading somewhere that Roman eulogists, when they celebrated and reanimated the dead grandee, would rely on a sequence of rhetorical tropes and conventions. He was wise in this way, just in this way, brave in this way, virtuous in this way. And so the pitted, carbuncular face of the departed was mortared over with a smooth paste, the better to idealise and immortalise. But—and this is the point—it was a pattern of characteristics previously applied to others, and which would be recycled for the future distinguished dead. And therefore, you could not, in modern terms, "understand" him. How different perhaps from the subjects of modern biography, and from the living people around us. Or, quite possibly, not.

Whenever I thought about her past, it would resolve or reduce itself into the quest for the man in the double-breasted overcoat. That image Chris had supplied hung before me like a pictorial enigma. How might I track him down? It took numerous hours of deep thought to realise that EF would probably have had an address book, and though he would hardly be listed under M for MIDBO, his name had a high chance of being present there. Unless he was dead, of course; or rather, even if.

It was a small grey-cloth item, organised in a characteristic way. Friends and colleagues were entered in ink, in that hand which was midway between cursive and italic. Tradesmen and professionals were entered in pencil, their useful lifespan presumed temporary. Her family came under F, her neighbours under N. A proportion of those listed were enclosed by square pencil brackets. These would be the dead, treated in a kindlier way than merely having their names crossed out. I also found it strange to see my own name there, turning me into some kind of objective presence. It made me briefly wonder when some celestial hand was going to put square brackets round my existence.

I had, at least, a reasonable excuse for ringing people out of the blue. I was one of EF's former students who had stayed in touch with her. I was planning to write a short memoir because, as I'm sure you would agree, she was one of the most original people I'd met in my entire life. And then, if they seemed receptive, I would modestly suggest that I be allowed to come and visit them.

That was the theory anyway. I swiftly discovered that not everyone shared my enthusiasm for EF; also, that a telephone call out of the blue could seem an impertinence; while others acted as if my modesty and caution were an indicator of unprofessionalism. It was true that I lacked the ruthlessness of a proper researcher. Responses varied from "Call me back if and when you have a contract—no, don't call me, write me a letter," to "Well, I barely remember her but if you'd like to drop round for coffee one morning"—this from someone living 250 miles away. At times I was almost tempted to say, "Let me cut to the chase—do you now, or have you ever, owned a double-breasted overcoat? And were you the love of her life?"

Years ago, I had an actor friend who, finding himself in new company, and as the night wore on, would sometimes ask those left: "Have you ever had your heart broken?" Some would remember they had an early start in the morning; others would reply that this was private business, thank you very much. Hesitating pedants might delay examination by asking for definitions, for terms and conditions. But I admired my friend for his transgressive move, and those who stayed, whether frank by nature or emboldened by drink, would often produce an exchange of hushed intensity, aided by the obvious willingness of their quizmaster to lay before them the manner and frequency with which his own heart had been broken.

I sometimes wondered how Elizabeth Finch would have

reacted to such an invitation. Some might think this woman of grace and poise would smilingly depart for bed. But my guess is that she would have responded to my friend's openness with equal candour. And that listeners would be staggered by what she said: not staggered by how and whom she had loved, but by her clarity of vision and lack of self-pity.

As I imagine it. The man in the double-breasted overcoat. Elizabeth Finch's—dare I even apply the adjective to her— kittenish behaviour. That of a lover, to be sure. And this was clearly not the start, or the end, of their relationship. Nor was it like catching them *en flagrant délit*, as she herself might have put it. I asked Christopher about luggage, he said he couldn't remember; but given that brother and sister then had lunch together, he would surely have noticed an overnight bag if she had one with her.

She puts her hands out, palms down. He places his hands, palms up, beneath hers. She uses his support to raise herself on tiptoe, while her other leg, almost of its own volition, bends at the knee and sticks out behind her, like a flamingo's. It is clearly not a one-off gesture; it is how they say goodbye— and doubtless hello as well ... And it has already become a fixed image in my head. Not a fixed image as if I had witnessed the scene myself—more as if I was examining a photograph or grainy video loop. It ends with her watching him as he walks away.

This might be the end of a snatched meeting. He is a busy man. The place is an anonymous concourse, somewhere they are unlikely to be spotted; yet they take the risk of Christopher turning up early. I conclude that the man is married, or at least involved with someone else. He hasn't much time. She is deeply in love with him. She looks longingly after him as he walks off.

Or perhaps the opposite. He has dashed across town to snatch a brief espresso with her before she sees Chris. He is deeply in love with her. They have just shared a few golden moments in an otherwise dismal day. When he walks off, he doesn't turn and look at her because he is by nature discreet and cautious. *Or,* he doesn't turn because leaving her, even if he is to see her again tomorrow—even if they have a foreign trip planned involving a first-class couchette—is so painful that turning for a final glimpse would only exacerbate the pain. He might sob; he might howl publicly. And he is far less capable of stoicism than she.

We ask—or rather, I wonder—why, if she was such a stoic, did she ask her doctor to euthanise her when the time came. Aren't stoics meant to bear stoically whatever happens to them? Or maybe I'm confusing them with those Christians who believe that everything is the Lord's will, and they must bear the pains of dying because it is part of His plan for them. A divine plan which includes a few thousand more tormenting, ever-failing breaths, plus pain which morphine cannot counter, and mortal terror, all so that they will come to understand the Lord's purpose for them as they inherit the earth and are welcomed into the celestial embrace ("Thou hast conquered ..."). No, in Elizabeth Finch's philosophy, there are some things which are up to us, and some things that are not up to us. A stoic has agency: this dying is unbearable, and pointless, and a great waste of everyone's time, including her own, so she proposes—no, demands—that we agree to put an end to it. Except that she no longer has agency—which has passed into other hands, a power of attorney transferred with her acquiescence. And then there is the fortune or misfortune of whose medical hands we fall into.

This is not my story, as I may have mentioned. My life has been interesting to me at the time, but of little objective interest to anyone else. It has followed a predictable graph-line of expectation and disappointment, repeatingly. But I would say one thing: that famous quote about all happy families being happy in the same way, and all unhappy families being different from one another. I've always thought he got it the wrong way round. Most unhappy families I've seen—including two of my own—have been unhappy according to pretty repetitive formulae; whereas happy families, far from being some complacent norm, are often the result of active, individual character and effort. But there is also a third category: families pretending to be happy, or falsely remembering that they had once been happy: "Getting our history wrong is part of being a family!" Whereas I don't imagine there are families who are happy but falsely claim to be unhappy. However, this is straying off the path a little.

To return to it: a few days later, I had a further thought about Jewishness. EF was indeed telling the truth; it was her brother who was lying. Yes, Chris, the ever-so-English one, the fair-haired one, the countrified one, the deliberate avoider of high thought and high culture, the drinky, equable fellow who lived in an Essex village and jokily offered to drop his trousers. He, not she, was the fraud. No, that's too condemning a term. Rather, he was the sibling who was self-constructed, who, in EF's terms, established his own authenticity through artifice. Though if I had put it to him like that, he would have done his baffled, all-above-my-head-chum act, which had completely taken me in, as it was intended to.

And then I think some more. I prefer to believe EF. After all, she always told the truth. Except when she didn't. For instance, when Chris had asked her who the man in the double-breasted overcoat was, and she replied, "Oh, that? That was *nobody.*" Clearly untrue; though has anyone never told a lie in matters of love and sex? I suppose it all comes down to what and who you believe. And death changes things. Posthumous belief somehow cements authenticity.

It happened like this. She wrote occasionally for the *London Review of Books.* They had started a series of public lectures, and invited her to contribute. They offered her a fee; she declined it while laying down a single condition: that the event not be recorded in any way. She believed that such occasions were special: though "public," they were also private. People would have made an effort to come and hear her; and so in reply, she would be talking only to them. This may have been naivety on her part. But then, she was not always as worldly as she had seemed to her students.

I found out about it through a small ad. Naturally, EF would never have said to me, "By the way, I am giving a public lecture, and would be cheered by your presence." She would have regarded such a request as not just pitiful but also manipulative, an interference in my life.

She had wanted to call the lecture "Thou Hast Conquered, O Pale Galilean," but the *LRB* had gently edited it into "Where Do Our Morals Come From?" I sat well out of her eyeline and put my head on one side. It was like being back in her classroom, but without the anxiety. This time, I knew the story in advance. She began with Julian's death in the Persian desert and how it was a disaster for paganism and Hellenism. The triumph—and the catastrophe—of monotheism. How the dominance and corruption of Christianity led to "the closing of the European mind." How Julian was morally superior to a whole succession of popes. How joy— yes, she did say "joy" specifically—had leached out of Europe, except for permitted pagan survivals such as Carnival. The tyrannous nature of both Catholicism and Protestantism. The shameful persecution and expulsion of Jews and Muslims. Her fundamental belief that the source of our moral attitudes and behaviour lay further in the past than most of us were aware; unfortunately, not as far back as the brief reign of Julian the Apostate.

Her lecture would not normally have attracted any press coverage; perhaps the *Times*'s elderly classics correspondent might have filed a few hundred words. But it was summer, Parliament was in recess, for once no wars involving British troops were taking place, nor were there any unsolved kidnappings of small children. It was the silly season for journalists. And there was also the fact that the *London Review of Books* was viewed with great suspicion by elements of the right-wing press, who saw it as a nest of leftists, subversives, pseudo-intellectuals, cosmopolitans, traitors, liars and anti-monarchist vermin. We must also factor in the historic English delight of publicly indulging in fits of morality.

The headline read "CRAZY LADY" PROF CLAIMS

ROMAN EMPERORS RUINED OUR SEX LIFE. You can easily imagine how EF's sober facts and speculations were turned into scandalous matter. For instance, the poet Swinburne was a known homosexual with a taste for flagellation: was that the prof's idea of an honourable English gentleman whose views were worth considering? For instance, what on earth did she mean by "the closing of the European mind" when it had produced Shakespeare, Leonardo da Vinci, Dante, Beethoven, Darwin, Isaac Newton and so on? Not to mention Monty Python, an instructive contrast to the said humourless "Crazy Lady." As for the notion that what you got up to in bed was somehow affected by what long-dead Christians and popes had thought about it all was, in the words of one editorial commentator, "a load of bollocks."

The story had sudden traction. Elizabeth Finch was doorstepped and photographed as unflatteringly as possible. Reporters turned up an "ex-student" who claimed that EF had once "mocked" the wartime death of his father, had "grandstanded" about the deaths of her own relatives in concentration camps, while at the same time suggesting they read *Hitler's Table Talk*. Questions were asked such as: "Is your name really Elizabeth Finch?" (perhaps changed from Jessica Finkelstein?). Her attack on monotheism was characterised by one editorial thinker as "a commitment to the mongrelisation of our culture and civilisation typical of the cosmopolitan intellectual class. They boast of being citizens of the world, but are citizens of nowhere, and would turn all our beloved English parish churches into 'multifaith centres.'" One newspaper called for EF's dismissal from London University. When it was pointed out that she had retired several years previously, they called for the withholding of her pension. There was a *Guardian* leader about freedom of speech, while at the baser end of Fleet Street one paper ran a front page with two pictures side by side: one of EF, door-stepped, looking alarmed and tired, the other of a "glamour model" who had "once auditioned to be a Bond girl," and was soon to publish a book of her own "beauty secrets." The text below read: "We ask who looks as if they know more about Love and Sex: Prof. Liz or Luscious Linzi? You decide." There was a number to ring and "register your opinion." The *Guardian* pointed out that Linzi's publisher was owned by the same tax-avoiding non-resident billionaire as owned the newspaper. But few considered this central to the story.

EF herself said nothing; she asked the *London Review of Books* not to comment. They suggested bringing out her lecture as a pamphlet; she declined.

After the shitstorm had blown itself out, I wrote her a letter of ... what? Condolence? The tone was hard to find. Too much sympathy—or even exactly the right amount—might still somehow imply that she was a weak and feeble being. Also, one naive about the world's casual cruelty. Perhaps even one lacking the moral fortitude to survive what I came to think of as The Shaming.

To my surprise, she telephoned. This was a rare occurrence in a relationship mainly conducted by post and lunch.

"They choose to understand nothing," she said, quite calmly, as if being mocked and sneered at was a normal part of a retired academic's life. "It was kind of you to be upset on my behalf, but unnecessary. They choose to understand nothing." And then, her message delivered, she put the phone down, and the matter was never referred to again.

I can't prove that all this made her more—even more—

of a hermit. The pattern of her days had long been decided and did not vary. But she certainly never gave another lecture, and published nothing—not even a book review—thereafter.

Unable to discuss any of this with her, I returned to those key opening words of the *Handbook* of Epictetus. "Some things are up to us and some things are not up to us." The things that are up to us "are by nature free, unhindered, and unimpeded"; while the things that are not up to us are "weak, enslaved, hindered, not our own." You can only be free and happy if you recognise this essential difference between what you can change and what you can't. Among the things "not up to us" are "our bodies," "our possessions," "our reputations" and "our public offices." *Our reputations*.

And the second thing I thought was this: Regardless of the above, and of EF's known character and mentality, and words of response on the telephone, even so, even so, I regard what happened to her as a kind of martyrdom. You—and doubtless she—might view this as a rhetorical exaggeration. After all, no one died; nor did she wish to be either a victim or a myth. But a coarse public shaming, and a mockery of all she believed in, nonetheless. So I'll stick with martyrdom, if you don't mind.

A final thought. About The Shaming. EF withdrew, she was less in the world. But she was *not shamed*.

Years later, after her death, I brought the matter up over lunch with Chris. I approached it carefully, suspecting that the paper Chris read had initiated, or at least vigorously pursued, the story.

"When she got into that bit of trouble—you know, the

lecture she gave—did she talk to you about it? I mean, she wouldn't talk to me, and no reason why she should." My mock-modesty was a touch hypocritical, and unFinchian.

He was silent for a while. "I saw it in the papers, of course. I just skimmed the headlines. I didn't really follow it. Just thought, you bastards. What had Liz done to deserve that? I cancelled the paper—for a few weeks, anyway. Maybe you can explain what it was all about."

I was unprepared for this. I began expounding on Julian the Apostate and the Galileans, but he swiftly interrupted.

"No, I don't really want to know. I just thought it was really shitty, putting her picture next to some half-dressed totty hanging out of her swimsuit. I'm sure what Liz had to say was above their heads, anyway."

"Did you talk to her about it?"

"I dropped her a card. Didn't hear back for a week or so, which was unusual—she'd normally reply by return. Get it off her desk and into the wastepaper basket." Then he suddenly smiled. "Anyway, about ten days later I got a short letter. It was very Liz. She said she was sorry to have brought shame on the family—no, she didn't put it like that, she said she was 'pained to have blotted the family escutcheon' and hoped we wouldn't all be drummed out of the village. Well, not much chance of that. After all, Finch is a pretty common name, and as I said, she never showed her face in Essex, or hadn't done for years. Oh yes, and she signed it, 'Your sinning but unrepentant sister, Elizabeth.'"

"That sounds just like her."

"It was. It cheered me up, to tell you the truth. Showed the bastards hadn't ground her down."

"And afterwards?"

"Afterwards, I would still come up to town and share a

TT lunch. She carried on taking the kids out—though they were growing up by now."

"Just out of interest ... why did you put up with your lunches being alcohol-free? She wouldn't have minded you drinking."

He paused. "Because I got a kind of pleasure out of it. I don't *have* to drink at lunchtime, I just prefer it that way. And I liked the fact that it never crossed Liz's mind that I might want to. I'd sit there and think, 'You're cleverer than me and younger than me and I love you like a sister, but you don't know everything.' And that, in a funny way, made me love her more. It's an odd thing, life, don't you find?"

I agreed.

This last exchange (and its unexpected source) got me thinking about the secrecies of love; the not-showings and the not-tellings. I don't mean The Love That Dare Not Speak Its Name and suchlike, but the ordinary pleasures of—what?—a sort of chosen hiddenness. I've said that I loved Elizabeth Finch—at least, I'm fairly sure I did; and I still do, beyond the grave. It was a love that started in the classroom, but it wasn't the calf-love, the puppy-love that children feel for their teachers. I was in my mid-thirties, after all. It wasn't in any way like marital love—at least, not as I've experienced it. Nor was it a fantasy love, despite my mild sexual dreamings. (A confession: I used to think, in moments of lazy wondering, that in the unlikely event of our going to bed together, I would still call her "Elizabeth Finch"—both names. And in such loose dreams, I found that she would welcome this, and that, beneath the bedclothes, the formality of such an address would mutate, and those two words would take on an intimate, teasing, sexy colouration. Make of this what you will.) Nor was my love in any way delusional. I never spoke to her about it, of course; but had I done so, she might have reached across the table, as she had done with Linda, placing her hand beside mine, and answered, "It's the only thing there is." Which—I guess— would not have been a flirtatious encouragement, but rather a plain acknowledgement of an agreed fact.

And what category did my love for EF fall into? Well, I'd say that it was Romantic-Stoic, which was appropriate. And did I love her more than either of my wives? Put it this way: part of love is being surprised by the person you love, even if you know them deeply and well. It's a sign that love is alive. Inertia kills love—and not just sexual love; all kinds of love. In my experience, the "surprises" of marital love, after the first few years, sometimes turn out to be mere whimsicalities; worse, the expression of someone bored not just with her husband, but with herself—indeed, with life itself. Of course, I never understood this at the time. The surprises of EF were different. There are people who prefer books to life, who are wary of deeper, more unquiet involvements. I don't think I'm like that; but it's true that perhaps I preferred loving EF to loving anyone else I've known, before or since. I don't mean I loved her *more*—that wouldn't be plausible—but I loved her carefully: with care, and fully.

She was, quite simply, the most grown-up person I have met in my life. Perhaps I mean the only grown-up person. Of course she wasn't interested in football or celebrity chefs or the ever-changing dictates of fashion, or box sets or gossip. She had long ago decided her distanced level of interest in the normal bandwidths of human preoccupation (and no, she wasn't in any way a snob). She just took the longer, and the higher view. I remember we were discussing—no, I was ranting about—some minister who was held to have brought disgrace upon his office for one of the usual reasons. I paused, and asked her,

"I imagine that you despise politicians?"

"Whyever would you imagine that?"

"Because they're corrupt and self-seeking and vain and incompetent."

"I don't agree. I think most of them are well-meaning, or believe themselves to be. Which makes their moral tragedy all the more to be pitied."

Do you see what I mean? The shimmer of her phrasing, the lustre of her brain.

Another memory. Her eyes were brown, and seemed larger than other people's because they appeared to remain open all the time. I can't remember her blinking. It was almost as if to blink was to shut yourself off—lazily, fearingly—from the world, and to waste a millisecond or two of your life on this planet.

From EF's notebooks:

—Is there a word in the English language more mythified, more misused, more misunderstood, more flexible of meaning and intent, more tainted, more sullied by the spittle of a billion lying tongues, than the word "love"? And is there anything more banal than complaining about this? Yet for all its misuse, we cannot replace it, because at the same time it is robust, granitic, its armour impermeable. It is waterproof, stormproof, thunderbolt-deflecting.

I used to reread this entry from time to time, occasionally musing on what I took to be its universal truth. Then, not long ago, I cut out a newspaper article about a Korean woman who had escaped from the North to the South. She was talking about love. "If you grow up in the West," she said, "you may think romance occurs naturally, but it does not. You learn how to be romantic from books and movies, or from observation. But there was no model to learn from in my parents' time. They didn't even have the language to talk about their feelings. You just had to guess how your beloved felt from the look in his eyes, or the tone of her voice as she spoke to you."

Or: she lifts herself up, supported by his hands, until one leg is on tiptoe, and the other sticks out behind her, like a flamingo. It seems to me that at times we can all be North Koreans.

From my notebooks (if I had any):

—Describe your relationship to Elizabeth Finch in five words. "She was my advisory thunderbolt."

I took down her copy of *The Golden Legend*. I read about St. Ursula again, and then flicked the pages, looking for her lightly pencilled markings. A line, a tick, a cross—these were her only forms of commentary. Often, they draw attention to the normal human reactions of those who are not central figures in the litany of martyrdom. Here, for instance, is the case of two well-born brothers from Narbonne, who are avid for a holy death. Their mother, in a state of pre-grief, berates them like this:

Here is a novel way of dying, when the victim begs the executioner to strike, when he prays for his life to end, and beckons death to come! Here is a new grief, a new misery, when one's young sons forfeit their youth willingly, and parents are forced to live on in a pitiable age!

When their aged father adds his own pleas, followed by those of their two wives, the young men's resolve begins to wobble. Whereupon the future St. Sebastian enters to strengthen their morale, perform a miracle, and exalt the glory of martyrdom. His argument, marked with a double pencil line by EF, is a denunciation of life and an affirmation of death. "Ever since the world began," Sebastian claims, "life has duped those who put their faith in it, deceived those who sought it, mocked those who trusted it. It affords security to no one, but proves false to all." The best response is to get out as early as you can: the two brothers, asserting their faith the more strongly, are tied to a stake and run through with spears.

But these deaths are just precursors to Sebastian's own. Like the best martyrs, he first escapes several attempts to kill him. The most famous of these pre-death deaths is when the emperor Diocletian orders him to be tied to a tree and used for archery practice: "They hit him with so many arrows that he looked like a hedgehog" (aha, I thought, remembering EF's notebook—and here is a confirmatory tick in the margin) "and they left him there for dead." The scene is familiar from many art galleries, and I have always assumed—as did Diocletian's archers—that their arrows were the actual cause of death. In fact, St. Sebastian survived this hedgehoggery, and his gateway to martyrdom consisted instead of being beaten to death with clubs and thrown into a sewer. But the painters were right to illustrate the earlier segment of the story. I remembered EF's words: "One secret of the Christian religion's success was always to employ the best moviemakers."

Modern martyrs of an Islamicist persuasion strive to take out as many infidels as possible at their moment of blessed transformation. Christian martyrs were so persuasive that before their own martyrdoms they converted many others, urging them to queue-jump their way to paradise. Either way, I remembered EF's remark that "such desire for death is almost voluptuous."

Pagans like Julian the Apostate used animal sacrifices in the observance of their faith; and though his consumption of white bulls might appear excessive, you honoured the gods (and got them on your side) by giving them the best. If this seems primitive, then modern times might seem more primitive to those old pagans: for centuries we slaughtered bulls not for a theological purpose, but as part of a fee-paying, ticketed-entry spectacle.

Does civilisation progress? Elizabeth Finch liked to ask us that question. Undoubtedly it does in terms of medicine, science, technology. But in human, moral terms? In terms of philosophy? In terms of seriousness? In AD 400, EF told us, the English princess St. Ursula, along with her eleven thousand virgins, was massacred outside Cologne for the love of God and the hope of heaven. Doubtless the numbers were miscounted, but even so. In French the martyrs are known as *Les onze mille vierges*. Fifteen hundred years later, the poet Apollinaire wrote a pornographic novel called *Les onze mille verges*— a vowel is missing, and *verge* means penis—in which almost as much blood is spilt through flagellation, decapitation, and other sadistic sexual practices, as had flowed beneath the walls of Cologne.

I was daydreaming. I was in hospital. It was Christmas. A hospital visitor came towards my bed. I was surprised to see her, from the black brogues on her feet to the coiffed grey-blonde hair. She, it seemed, was not surprised to see me. She turned the chair around so that we were face-to-face. She put her hand out and rested it flat beside mine.

"How is that?" she asked, with an eager yet satirical tone. "Disappointing?"

Then, as in dreams, she disappeared, and though I knew her to be dead, her question was living. Though what it referred to I was unsure. To my life? To my dying? To death itself? Whichever, the ploy was classic EF: she asked a tantalisingly easy question which set you off on a train of thought, alone. For my death: it was, I suppose, a disappointment that I was unable to face it with indifference verging on contempt, as demonstrated by Julian the Apostate, Montaigne, many others I had read about, not to mention EF herself. For my dying, I suppose I was disappointed because it seemed merely a process to be undergone: pain, and the relief of pain, boredom and loneliness despite the professional sympathy offered; nor did I come close to forming any famous—or even interesting—last words. As for my life, had that been disappointing? Whether so or not, what did it matter now? I was going to no final judgement, and though theorists of mortality claim it is good for the dying to come to terms with what their life has been, to "understand their own story," I felt no such necessity. The King of Unfinished Projects was leaving this one unstarted. Though not all my projects have been failures. I had done proper remembrance to Elizabeth Finch. And if, like the ancients, I believed in dreams and portents, I might have concluded that her visitation was a sign of approval, an indication that what I had done had pleased her.

But now I was in danger of self-congratulation. So I left off daydreaming and went back to the rest of my life.

Despite myself, I carried on reading about Julian the Apostate; in a way, I couldn't let him go just as I couldn't let EF go. But I discovered a downside to this: not all that I had written was true. Rather than correct my original text, I have put here the following addenda:

—He wasn't called "Julian the Apostate" at first. Early Christian writers simply called him "the Apostate," which was one of several ways of referring to Satan. They held him to be the Devil incarnate. Only later did he acquire his full title, making it look as if his chief sin was to have rejected Christianity.

—I had assumed that the story of Julian's death by "a Christian lance" was the invention of Christian propagandists. But this wasn't the case: it was Julian's friend and biographer Libanius who first came up with the phrase. Unsurprisingly, Christian writers thereafter adopted it with enthusiasm.

—Another mistake, or unthinking misrepresentation: when I said that Julian "wrote and published" his satire The Beard-Hater, I didn't consider what that second verb might mean back then. I was imagining some kind of general distribution and the city of Antioch wincing at the emperor's attack. But "publication" consisted of merely this: the text being posted up at the Elephant Arch just outside the palace "for all to read and copy." How many did so, we cannot know—and in any case, the emperor and his army left the city soon after. The probability is that Julian wrote it mainly for his own satisfaction and that of his friends; in this, it resembles "the pseudo-speeches of late antiquity that were never delivered nor meant to be delivered."

—I have been referring to Christianity (as EF did) as a monotheism. After all, that's how we think of it now. But Hellenists regarded *Christianity* as polytheistic, because it came with a tripartite God—the Father, the Son and the Holy Ghost. A view which survived into seventeenth-century England: see "Julian" Johnson's dismissal of Roman Catholicism as "polytheistic."

—The story of St. Mercurius and St. Basil combining their metaphysical powers turns out to be "a late Christian invention." Furthermore, I discover, Mercurius himself, "like most of the early Christian martyrs," simply didn't exist.

And here we reach an important point. I suppose I've always instinctively (or idly) believed that those brilliant myths and martyrdoms, with their thumping messages of salvation, while doubtless being "improved" as they were told and retold, were rooted in some rougher original reality. When you look at a great painting of a violent martyrdom, it compels and convinces you as the representation of something that had once happened. But all those holy compilations, like *The Acts of the Christian Martyrs*, and their subsequent illustration, are mere edifying fictions rather than True Lives. Current opinion among scholars is not just that few of those famous martyrs ever existed, but the actual number of them was tiny. Of course, there were many Christians killed "simply" for being Christians (and refusing to deny their faith in a court of law); but again, far fewer than previously assumed. A "sober computation" concludes that in the first three centuries of the Christian era, "at least two and at most ten thousand Christians were executed by the temporal power of the Roman Empire." (So much for St. Ursula's eleven thousand!) As for the number of those who willingly sought their own deaths, in the sure and certain belief of being fast-tracked to heaven: "Even the Church Fathers can't produce more than one or two cases of voluntary martyrdom."

Further: we think (or I thought) that pagans killed Christians, and Christians pagans, on and on, back and forth, in tit-for-tat slaughterings. They did, but this was minor stuff compared to the violence between Christians of varying beliefs. (The narcissism of small differences.) As Ammianus said, they would fight "like wild beasts" when disputing among themselves, while Gibbon stated wryly, "It is a salutary reminder of the significance of theological exactitude that more Christians were put to death in a single year of the Christian Empire than had been executed in three centuries of pagan dominion."

I confess that all this initially disheartened me. But I took it on board and came up with two conclusions. First, that theologians can also make excellent novelists. And secondly, that getting its history wrong is part of being a religion. I also discovered more about the afterlife of St. Ursula. In the early twelfth century Cologne expanded beyond its old city walls; and in the course of excavations, a vast burial ground was discovered, containing tens of thousands of skeletons. The city was already a pilgrimage destination; now archaeology (if that isn't too advanced a term) had beautifully confirmed religious history. Furthermore, a dove miraculously indicated to a local bishop precisely which set of body remnants belonged to the saint. Thousands of skeletons and six hundred skulls were transported to the specially constructed Sankt Ursula Kirche. This consoling proof—the largest ossuary north of the Alps—became a centre of the Christian tourist trade for centuries. Alas, when DNA testing came along, the bones turned out to be approximately two thousand years old, and the site probably that of an old Roman burial ground. Undiscouraged, however, visitors still come like pilgrims to gaze upon the imposter relics.

Coming across Anna's name in EF's address book gave me a start. I'd lost touch with her not long after she'd gate-crashed that lunch: it had seemed a final provocation, whether deliberate or not. But that had been years ago. At some point she had moved back to Holland—there was an address for her in Alkmaar. I looked it up in my Michelin Green Guide. The cheese capital of Holland. A weigh-house. Canals, old houses, an art museum. Well, why not, I thought.

No email address, of course. I remembered how EF had compared the Internet to the railways. A beguiling convenience with no intrinsic moral value or effect. So I wrote Anna an old-fashioned letter: out of the blue indeed, saw her name in EF's address book (let her work that bit out for herself), was planning a trip to Amsterdam, perhaps I could take a bus or train up to Alkmaar. Have lunch, look at some pictures in memory of EF, buy some cheese . . . if not, maybe when she was next in London. I kept it bland. I remember how irritated she used to get by me. Irritated when she thought I was being pushy or selfish; but equally irritated when she thought I was being hesitant or wishy-washy. To Anna, I seemed to have no still centre, and therefore no instinctive moral locators. Well, that was one reading of me. I put my email address beneath my signature.

Being Anna, she left it until I had virtually given up hope. An email. She could meet me at one o'clock on any Thursday in September at the entrance to the art museum. No explanation of the choice of day or time. No "it'll be nice to see you again." Take it or leave it, now or never. So, in return, I decided to keep her waiting, and chose the last Thursday of the month.

London to Amsterdam via Brussels. I've always enjoyed long train journeys. I like to think about what food to take, and what book to read. And this time, I thought I'd found something very appropriate.

I had pretty much abandoned my research into Julian's posthumous fame when it reached modern times; when the Apostate became less a touchstone for wider cultural issues, and more a matter of personal response. Though to be honest, I was also wearying at the prospect of another trudge through familiar material. So Robert Browning's 1976 biography of Julian definitively let me off reading Dmitri Merezhkovsky's novel ("turgid in expression and confused in plot . . . it adds nothing to our understanding of Julian"); also Kleon Rangavis's "gigantic tragedy"—1,500 lines of prose and 9,000 of verse—which is "far too long to be staged, and even to read it demanded an unusual effort, since it was written in the most uncompromisingly classical Greek." I was interested to discover that the Apostate had been the subject of two operas, one by the Austrian conductor-composer Felix Weingartner (1928) and another by the Russian Lazare Saminsky (published 1959, though written in the 1930s). But I wasn't cast down to discover that neither had been recorded, let alone performed.

Even so, I would, occasionally and almost nostalgically, scroll through what I called my bibliography of the so-far-unread. And so I chanced upon Michel Butor's *La Modification* (1957), a notable product of the *nouveau roman*. As its English title, *Changing Track*, might imply, it all takes place on a train—indeed, several trains. Not London to Amsterdam—that would be asking too much—but Paris to Rome, and vice versa. It concerns Léon Delmont, senior manager at a typewriter manufacturer, who is oscillating both geographically and emotionally between his wife and family in Paris and his lover in Rome. The novel consists of Delmont's memories and anticipations, his imaginings and his doubts, as he sits on a variety of trains between the two cities. I should perhaps add that the novel is written in the second person, which some might find annoying.

The book begins well for Apostasologists:

p. 14 The early-morning train from Paris pulls out past empty pavements and closed shops, the Sorbonne church, and "the ruins that are known as the Thermae of Julian the Apostate, although they are probably older than the emperor." Indeed, my old *Baedeker Guide to Paris* (1911) confirms that they are the remnants of a palace built between 292 and 306 by the emperor Constantius Chlorus and are where "Julian was proclaimed emperor by his soldiers in 360."

p. 61 The narrator remembers walking "deliberately, like a tourist, along the boulevard Saint-Germain" . . . and then past "those walls of brick and stone, the remains of the Thermae that Julian the Apostate knew, and the only significant relics of his 'beloved Lutetia,' which amply justifies the attribution of his name to them."

p. 81 The action hots up. The narrator is now leaving Rome for Paris. "You settled down in your compartment . . .

and you immersed yourself in *The Letters of Julian the Apostate*."

Naturally, the reader will now start to wonder about the connection between the manager of the typewriter firm and the Roman emperor. An idea strikes: perhaps it's the case that for a married man to abandon his wife and children and run off with his lover is a kind of apostasy? And the Delmont family are practising Catholics. What could there be in Julian's letters which might respond to, or affect, the main plot?

p. 168 On another train (it seems). "You took up once more *The Letters of Julian the Apostate* which you had left on the shelf, but you held the book in your hands without opening it, looking through the open window which sometimes let in a whiff of sand on the cool breeze . . ."

Some readers might find the suspense unbearable. When will the reveal take place? There are only sixty pages to go.

p. 169 "HOLDING ON YOUR KNEES THE CLOSED VOLUME OF *THE LETTERS OF JU-LIAN THE APOSTATE*, WHICH YOU HAD FIN-ISHED READING." The outraged capital letters are mine. Or maybe Butor is just teasing us (the *nouveau roman* had its ludic side), and all will be disclosed at the death.

p. 208 Time is getting short now. "You were alone, holding the emperor Julian's letters in your hand, having left the suburbs of Genoa behind." Think, think: there must be some connection between the two men. Perhaps it is the contrast between the Parisian adulterer and the chaste Julian, who strode untainted through the fleshpots of Antioch and disdained the beautiful female captives of his Persian campaign? Not that Butor has mentioned the emperor's private life; or, indeed, anything about him.

p. 215 "You set down your suitcases [in your Rome hotel room] on the table AND TOOK OUT VOLUME I OF THE *AENEID* IN THE BUDÉ EDITION." This is beyond a joke: authorial insolence, I would call it.

p. 225 "Sitting by the window [of your Paris apartment], you were taking the letters of Julian the Apostate from your bookcase when Henriette [your wife] came in to ask if you'd be there for dinner." But you prefer to dine on the train. And here we have a reprise:

p. 225 It is pitch-dark and raining, so you take a taxi to the station. It "turned round the corner of the ruined palace attributed to the Parisian emperor."

And that is it, in terms of Julian. And that was pretty much it, in terms of me. A few pages later, the reader—you—is informed that the narrator—also you—is planning to write a novel about his (your) emotional dilemma to make sense of it. And guess what? The novel you have just read is the very novel that the typewriter manager (also you) turns out to have written!

It seemed appropriate that my time with Julian's afterlife should end on such a diminuendo. And my time with Elizabeth Finch was also coming to an end. It felt a long way from that meeting with Christopher in EF's beige and brown flat in West London, from scrabbling in her desk and imagining novelettishly that she had bequeathed an unfinished masterpiece for me to curate. She had left me something far more real and far more elusive: an idea to follow. Whether I have followed it correctly, I cannot tell—only she would know that.

I spent a couple of days in Amsterdam, then caught a mid-morning train to Alkmaar. I had booked into a hotel just outside the centre of town. I walked to the art museum, trying not to arrive excitedly early or annoyingly late—though with Anna you could also be annoyingly punctual. She, as if in parody, turned up at the same moment. This being Europe, I felt it safe to kiss her on the cheek.

"We've both gone grey," I said.

"It suits me better than you. And I went grey by choice." But she was half-smiling, so I laughed.

There was a special exhibition of Caesar van Everdingen—"Alkmaar's Rembrandt," as he was known. It included several vast canvases of the town's Old Civic Guard, a portrait of a cute two-year-old boy holding a goldfinch (on loan from Barnsley, to my surprise), a moral scene of Diogenes Looking for an Honest Man in a contemporary local setting, and a portrait of a Dutch East India Company trader with two black slaves. These images were all familiar to me because I'd ordered a copy of the catalogue before coming to Alkmaar. We stood in front of Diogenes the Cynic holding up a lantern in broad daylight, to emphasise the fruitlessness of his search. The picture included a wheelbarrow full of turnips in reference to the philosopher's frugal diet; while even the dog in the foreground alluded to the philosopher—the Greek for dog being *kuon*, from which the word "cynic" is also derived. Anna was suspicious of such unexpected knowledge, but didn't query it. Pointing to the barrowful of turnips, I said,

"Elizabeth Finch certainly wouldn't have made a Cynic."

"Let's just look at the pictures, shall we?"

"I only know this stuff because I got the catalogue sent to me in England."

"Oh, you are *hopeless*," Anna replied crossly. Hopeless at any form of deviousness, I took her to mean. This was true. And I'd already shown my hand by referring to EF. Though as a shrink might have pointed out, perhaps my deviousness lay in appearing not to be devious: being hopeless was my form of cunning.

We looked at the pictures.

They say—or rather, "they say"—Never Go Back, don't they? Don't chase that missed love, that half-forgotten love, that misunderstood love years later. If it went wrong the first time, it'll go wrong the second time. And so on. But I wasn't Going Back, not in that sense (as far as I knew, anyway). I had a different purpose. And so, as we sat with a dish of vivid melted cheese and a glass of wine in a sunlit cobbled square, we found it easy to be with one another. Anna worked as a translator; she'd been in Alkmaar for six years, moving from Amsterdam for unspecified reasons. She wore no wedding ring; I didn't ask. I told her about my life, my second divorce, what my children were up to. She was hardly full of prompts and questions; but she seemed relaxed in my presence. We talked some more about Caesar van Everdingen, lamented the Brexit vote, and so on.

"I'm thinking of writing about Elizabeth Finch. A tribute of some sort. I find I still miss her."

She didn't, as I'd half-expected, say, "I thought as much," or even, as I would have feared, "But *you* can't write." Instead, she merely nodded and said, "Me too." She meant the missing, not the writing.

At first, we just evoked her: clothes, poise, wit, rigour. What she taught us whether on the syllabus or (more likely) off it. What remained with us.

"Ursula and her eleven thousand virgins," I said.

"Suicide by Cop," she replied instantly, and we laughed, looking at one another, warmly, while assessing time's damage.

"Julian the Apostate," I proposed.

"Don't remember him."

"The last pagan emperor. She called his death 'the moment history went wrong.'"

"I'd have remembered that, surely. I can only remember some other Julian who said sex was cool and original sin a rubbish idea."

I thought this very Dutch of her.

"Hmm. Actually, you may be right—maybe it was in one of her notebooks. I sometimes get confused between memory and research." I told her a bit about Julian, though not that I seemed to be writing as much about him as about EF.

"Were you still in England at the time of The Shaming, as it was called?"

Anna had left by then, though was still in touch with EF, who naturally had not mentioned it in any of her letters. I filled her in; she listened intently.

"That's disgusting," she said. "Your focking British newspapers."

"Yes. And I won't say she stopped work as a result. But she certainly stopped lecturing and book-reviewing."

"Did she leave anything she planned to publish?"

"Not really." I told her about the missing notebooks, and my speculations. "Perhaps she'd even tried to write a novel," I ended.

"I very much doubt that."

"No, you're right." I didn't know how to get past the preliminaries. Just plunge in, I told myself.

"Do you mind if I ask you some questions?"

"Go ahead."

"OK, long shot, but did she ever talk to you about a man in a double-breasted overcoat?"

Anna burst out laughing. "Very Sherlock Holmes." I liked that. I liked being teased. It brought things back. We talked about the class, and who we remembered, and who we liked and disliked.

"She was very kind to us," I said. "Do you remember Linda?"

"Sure," said Anna, but her face seemed to change a bit.

"She was always having heart trouble, as she called it. I remember her asking me if she should consult EF about it. I advised against, but she went on with it anyway. And EF said this wonderful thing to her: 'It's all that matters. It's the only thing.'" I quoted it, perhaps a little smugly.

"You're such a dunderwit," Anna said crossly. "Haven't changed in that respect, have you? Linda, poor Linda, was consulting, as you put it, EF, about *you*."

"Me? Fuck. Why … why didn't she tell me? Why didn't anyone tell me?" I was also thinking: "dunderwit," I like the coinage. "Oh fuck," I repeated, "I'll need some time to absorb that."

"Well, you've got the rest of your life," commented Anna heartlessly, as it seemed to me.

I didn't know what to say, except, "Can we continue this later? Over supper? I'm staying the night."

"Sure," she said. "I'll get lunch, you get dinner."

There seemed to be something a little triumphant in her tone.

I went back to my hotel room and lay on the bed. I thought about men and women, and how some of them always have to be helped over the stile, as it were.

After we had ordered, I took out my notebook, and was reaching into my jacket for a biro when she said, "No, I don't want that."

"But—"

"It makes her dead."

"But—"

"I said I'd talk to you about her. I'll do that. But if you were writing it all down in front of me I'd feel . . . a betrayer. Do you understand?" I didn't, but I nodded. "It makes her dead," she repeated. "And I don't want that. And she hasn't given me permission. Anyway, you'll remember what's important."

I paused, hoping she might explain more, or even change her mind. But she just pointed to my notebook, so I put it away.

What followed made it clear that Anna knew EF better than I did—at least when it came to the private, intimate dimension. I could hardly contest that, though I allowed myself to feel envy.

"You know how she was," Anna began. "A mixture of utter candour and sudden concealment. Also, utter sympathy and occasional distance. Talking to her was completely different from any other woman I've talked to in my life. Most women tell you How We Met"—she did air-quotes—"and What Went Wrong and How It Ended and What I Learnt From It All. I'm not disparaging that: I do it myself—turn my life into a story. We all do it. EF wasn't like that. She'd give you the conclusion but not the narrative. Why? The obvious, normal reason would be a sense of privacy, of discretion. But I decided that it was also perhaps something bigger: a sense that a life, much as we would like it to be, does not amount to a narrative—or not a narrative such as we understand and expect."

I love listening to women who are more intelligent, or more lucid, than me. And it made me remember the year

Anna and I were together. But that wasn't helpful in the present moment.

"So, um, could you give me an example of that?"

"She once said to me, 'I seem in my life to have specialised in either the unattainable or the undesirable.'"

I smiled automatically as EF's voice came through loud and clear.

"Did she specify? Any names?"

"Wait. There's something else, which has always haunted me. I wrote it down at the time." She pulled a folded paper from her bag. "'Love is always a mixture of the visceral and the theoretical. Of course, we do not recognise the theoretical as much—it is far too rooted in history and kinship. But this is why love is essentially artificial. I use that word in the best sense, of course. And what we call romantic love is the most artificial of all. And therefore the highest form, and also the most destructive.'"

"Blimey," I said. "No wonder both my marriages failed."

"Ah," Anna replied, "the old British facetiousness in the face of love. How I remember that. Male facetiousness, I mean."

"You think women are better? At love?" I have no especial loyalty to my own sex, but her certainty made me defensive.

"Of course. We are both more visceral and more high-minded."

I decided not to rise to this. "And do you think this was EF's view as well?"

"I'm not sure."

"Perhaps the visceral ones in her life were undesirable and the high-minded ones unattainable. Or the other way round." I imagined the man in the double-breasted overcoat to have been of the high-minded variety.

"So," I said, "this may seem like a banal question, but do you think she was ever happy?"

I half-expected Anna to castigate me for the triteness of my question. But she didn't.

"I'm not sure she believed that happiness was the natural or even the desirable consequence of love. I think she believed that love was more about truth than happiness. I remember she once said, 'Now that love is all in my past, I understand it better, both the clarity and the delirium.'"

I balked at such abstractions. How can you seek love and yet not want happiness? I preferred the specifics. "Can you give me any names?"

"I never knew them. And if I did I'm not sure I'd tell you. Why should they be bothered now? Old guys having their falsely happy memories disturbed by you."

"Any clues?"

"No shit, Sherlock."

I smiled. Anna had always possessed a taste for the confident misuse of slang. She was also—being a European—more at ease with the abstract and the theoretical than me. I remembered struggling as EF would gently instruct us in the thoughts of Epictetus and the Stoics.

"What was that thing she used to quote about some things being up to us ..."

"'There are those things that are up to us, and there are those things that are not up to us.'"

"Go on."

"And that we should learn to distinguish between them, and realise that there is nothing to be done about what is not up to us, and recognising this leads us to a proper philosophical understanding of life."

"And happiness?" I asked.

"I think the Stoics thought that a proper understanding of life was what other, less philosophical people—like you and me—might call happiness."

I was glad she included us on equal terms—even if those of inadequacy.

"So understanding is the highest good?"

"Of course."

"OK, then answer me this. Is love something that is up to us or something that is not up to us? What would EF have said about that?"

Anna paused. "I think she would have said that most people imagine it is up to them but that in reality it is not at all."

"And we should recognise this if we want to live a true philosophical life—which, let's face it, most people couldn't give a stuff about. Plus which, it's getting a bit late in the day for us to sign up to it."

"Yes."

"And EF recognised that love is not up to us?"

"Certainly."

"And therefore believed that love can bring only under-standing and not happiness? Or, perhaps, that happiness is contingent, not necessary?"

"Neil, we'll make a philosopher of you yet."

"Don't be alarmed. It's only the drink."

"Dutch beer is known to be good for the brain."

"Do you think she was ever a lesbian?"

"Thank you for reverting to type. To English type."

"Well, what am I meant to do about that? I am English, after all."

"Then fight against it?"

"Have *you* ever been a lesbian?"

"Fock the fock off," she said lightly. Now that was one of the phrases Anna never used incorrectly.

"I'm just trying to imagine EF in love."

"Don't try. You haven't the imagination."

"And you do?"

"Maybe, but it's not something I'm particularly interested in."

"Lesbianism?"

"No, posthumous and reductive gossip about a wonderful woman who's dead."

"I don't think trying to understand someone is at all the same as gossip."

"Then I'll leave you in that blissful state of ignorance."

This was just how our quarrels used to start. But I declined to feel nostalgic. I merely felt the same old tired irascibility. There are some things that are up to us, and Anna was not one of them. Nor could I see that if this were the case, it would lead me to an understanding of life and philosophical happiness. I've always been suspicious of paths of enlightenment, however seemingly rational.

"When did she say that thing?"

"What thing?"

"About understanding love better now that it was behind her."

"Five or six years before she died."

"So do we assume she was still in the game—pardon the expression—when she was teaching us?"

"Pass."

"Would you let me read her letters to you?"

"Of course not."

"Coffee and a schnapps?"

"Perfect."

And so we regained a balance of affability. No, more than that on my part. I was still very fond of Anna, however it might seem.

"Sometimes, when I think of EF, I feel as if I've let her down."

"In what way? After all, you're doing this ... research on her."

"Well, who knows if she'd even approve of that. No, it's more that, despite her continuing presence, even influence, I just carried on living my life in much the same old muddled way as I always had."

Anna took me seriously; she could see that I wasn't merely being self-indulgent.

"EF was very forgiving," she said. "For all her high standards."

"Yes, but I don't want to be *forgiven*. Do you see?"

She patted my forearm across the table. "Yes, Neil, I see."

Outside the restaurant, a quiet Dutch rain was drifting around. I took her arm. "Well, thank you for that." In reply, she slightly pushed herself against my shoulder, as if to say ... what?

Emboldened by the gesture, and by the schnapps, I said, "Is there any reason why we can't or shouldn't go to bed together?"

"Yes," she replied. "The way you just phrased that."

I laughed. Fair enough. Crassness isn't only the property of youth.

But she didn't take offence, and there she was, at the cafe on the cobbled square, happy to have a final coffee before I took the train back to Amsterdam.

"I was just remembering," she said, "what a good swimmer she was."

"Swimmer?"

"Yes, swimmer. She was a good one." Anna had an irritating half-smile, as if to say, I know things about her that you don't. No, cancel that "as if."

I tried to picture the scene and failed.

"You mean, Brighton Beach?"

"No, the Sanctuary."

"What's that?"

"Swimming pool and spa. Covent Garden—well, it's been closed a few years now. Women only. We used to go there once a month before I moved back."

I felt strangely blindsided by this. I had a sudden, half-shameful memory. When I was first describing EF, I said that she never showed bare legs, and you couldn't imagine her in beachwear.

"And . . . what was her swimming costume like?"

Anna laughed openly. "Well, it wasn't a bikini." At which I felt an absurd sense of relief. "But I'll let you into a secret, Neil. Some women have more than one swimsuit."

"Yes, of course. I think I'll have a schnapps with my coffee."

It was juvenile, and ridiculous. I'd already admitted to myself—well, I'd been forced to—that Anna might know more about EF's private life than I did. And here I was feeling jealous about . . . swimming. And swimsuits. In the old days, I would have sulked, and Anna would have teased me about sulking; but I wasn't going to give her that pleasure ever again.

"Still," she said brightly, "if you really are going to write about her, you'll have to show the other side."

"What other side?"

"Oh, come on." She took a sip of my schnapps without asking.

"Come on what?"

"Don't forget you were in love with her. In your own muddled, troubled way."

"It wasn't like that," I protested. Then, defiantly, "But it's true that I loved her. So did you."

"Differently, but yes. And I have no problem with that."

"And I do?"

"Oh yes. But more to the point, would you trust a biography written by the subject's lover?"

"It's not *exactly* a biography. And I wasn't her lover in that sense."

"Fine, but have you thought of, say, tracking down Geoff?"

"Geoff? That pile of right-on shite? Why the fuck would I want to do that?"

"The other side."

"The other side? The other side, as I recall, consisted *only* of Geoff."

"Remember what she said in that first class? Something like 'I might not be the best teacher for all of you.' She was for you and me. But not for some of the others. They wanted something more traditional. Dates, names, facts, all leading to broader ideas. Not broader ideas leading to dates, names, facts. Of course, they were intrigued to begin with, but then she became . . . unsettling."

"Exactly. She unsettled me—and you—as in, shook my mind around, made me constantly rethink, burst stars inside my head."

Anna smiled at me in rather too pointedly indulgent a way. "Yes, those starbursts. But a number of the class thought she was on top of her hobbyhorse all the time."

"Riding. Riding her hobbyhorse."

"Whatever. They wanted to pass exams and get on with, or back to, their lives."

"The more fool them."

"Neil, the inspirational teacher is a bit of a comfortable myth. It may be true for adolescents, but not for a group of thirty-year-olds. And you've always looked for women who can tell you what's what. Like me, for a while."

I was baffled, then outraged. Anna seemed to be confusing two entirely different parts of my life.

"So you think you're like EF?" I asked resentfully, meaning: as good as, as original as, as wonderful as.

"Neil, we've both got grey hair, it's too late in life to take offence."

"I'm not so sure about that. But you obviously think of yourself as someone who can tell the world what's what. I don't *need* it now. And we seem to be getting miles off the point."

"But we aren't."

"So are you now denying that EF was one of the most extraordinary people you ever met?"

"Not at all. She was. All I'm suggesting—without telling you what's what—is that it shouldn't be a monologue of praise. Remember what EF thought of mono words."

"Sure. Monologues are monotonous and monomaniacal and . . ."

". . . monocultural."

We laughed. It was still OK, we were still OK as friends.

"But you're not suggesting, are you, that I talk to Geoff?"

"I've got his email."

"Bloody hell." An unnerving thought crossed my mind. "You're not . . . you didn't . . . Geoff?"

She winked at me. Actually, she didn't ever get winking right, just as she didn't always get certain vernacular English phrases right. It came out halfway between a wink and a blink.

"You men," she just said. "You Englishmen."

I returned home with a large hunk of cheese and a few post-cards of works by "Alkmaar's Rembrandt." In a spirit of defiance against Anna (while also realising that I was following her advice), I turned on my computer.

Dear Geoff, This will probably seem a bit out of the blue. I saw Anna in Alkmaar and she gave me your address. I'm thinking of writing a short memoir about Elizabeth Finch. I wonder if you have any stories, anecdotes, particular memories? Also, whether what you thought about her has changed over the years. You may not want to be quoted, of course, or you might prefer me to redact your name. Let me know. Best wishes, Neil.

Two days later:

Dear Neil, Yes, she was quite a character, wasn't she, Old Finchy? She certainly had, I don't know what to call it, style, a way of presenting herself, which not many teachers do. I didn't mind that. And she knew a lot of stuff, to be sure, though it's always easier teaching a foundation course. She struck me as not so much old-school as antique-school. I know you had me tabbed as a mad Trot, but her view of what culture and civilisation were was totally untouched by modern thought, by systematic thought, by critical and intellectual theory. She was always going on about "rigour," but it seemed to me her teaching style was more about self-indulgence. She obviously thought of herself as "original"; I think a better word would be "amateur." And the days of the amateur scholar are long gone, my friend. I certainly used her as a counter-example when I became a lecturer. Do you remember her advising us to read Hitler? And she seemed obsessed by the early Christian Church. She wouldn't be able to get away with all that nowadays. I'm not saying she did much harm, just that her approach to everything, and her "quirky opinions," were somehow irrelevant. I'm quite happy for you to quote any of this, if you like. And good luck finding a publisher! Onward and upward, Geoff.

PS. At this distance in time, I'm sure you won't mind me saying that not only were you a bit potty about her, but you made her into a myth. Not that it does any harm, really. We all need our little myths to live by, don't we?

It was that "little" which got to me—plus the cheesy way he called me "my friend." What a steaming pile of horseshit, I thought. Also, he virtually admitted that he was the source of that tabloid story about EF and Hitler. At least he didn't suggest a reunion drink to "catch up on old times."

I had to concede that Anna was still good at reading me, after all these years. For instance, her clever peacemaking reference to the monologue. I remembered what EF said on the subject. "I do not deny its brilliance as a theatrical device. I merely wish to point out its extreme artificiality, which is, of course, the source of its brilliance." Not something I had ever thought about in my own modest career as an actor.

I realised that apart from her general legacy to me, EF had also left specific legacies: of words and phrases, of ideas which I couldn't necessarily understand or reconcile, but which would follow me down the years.

Another thing about my visit to Anna. Something she said left me wondering whether, beneath the calm, controlled face EF showed to the world, there might be an undercurrent—no, more like a a howling watercourse—of rage. This may be quite wrong. But then, I remember my surprise when one of my wives went to a homeopath and asked if there was a remedy for her ongoing condition, which she described as "seething resentment."

A recent biographer of Julian concluded that all his grand projects had failed, and that even his apparent victories—military, administrative, theological—were brief, even illusory. "Indeed, the 'mighty warrior's' only real victory was in cleaning up the tax system." Which made me remember EF proposing that failure can be more interesting than success, and losers tell us more than winners. Also, how we cannot tell, even on our deathbed—perhaps especially on our deathbed—how we will be judged, or, if at all, remembered. We might leave a footprint in the sand which the next wind blows away. Or we might leave a footprint in the dust, and a perfect cast of it will survive for centuries because we happen to live in Pompeii. When I think of Linda—despite Anna's corrective interference decades on—I know that I shall always remember her by that damp palm-print she left on a table in the college bar. Alone, I had downed first my drink and then hers, and by the time I stood up to go her palm-print had disappeared, and has not existed since, except in my stubborn memory.

I thought of Julian, and how the centuries had interpreted and reinterpreted him, like a man walking across a stage pursued by different-coloured spotlights. Oh, he was red, no, more like orange, no, he was indigo verging on black, no, he was all black. It seems to me, if in a less dramatic and extreme way, that this is what happens when we look at anyone's life: how they are seen by their parents, friends, lovers, enemies, children; by passing strangers who suddenly notice a truth about them, or by long-term friends who hardly understand them at all. And then they look at us, in a manner different from how we look at ourselves. Well, getting our history wrong is part of being a person.

At this late stage, I could acknowledge that there were some, like Geoff, who didn't rate EF; and others who wanted something different from her. I could also admit that some—perhaps many—in our class would have forgotten all about her over the years, or reduced her to a single, comic anecdote.

But I didn't care at all. Because, you see, it made her more *mine*.

Back to the starting point: Elizabeth Finch standing before us, speaking almost in written prose, having no perceptible gap between brain and tongue, poised, elegant, alarming, complete. Was she a confected person, one who had worked over the years on a manner of self-presentation until it was immaculate? Artificial, in other words. Yet such artificiality was at the service of authenticity. That's what she implied, indeed said. Does that make sense? We can all think of people who use a confected or artificial simplicity as a way of getting through the world. *Faux naïf*, we would call it. EF was neither false nor naive, indeed, at the opposite end of the spectrum; though still on it.

Put it like this. I had watched EF in the lecture hall, across the room at parties (from which she would always escape early), and over many lunches. She had been my friend, and I had loved her. Her presence and example had made my brain change gear, had provoked a quantum leap in my understanding of the world. I had read the notebooks she would have shown to nobody else; I had examined each pencil mark in the books she had left me. But perhaps all these meetings and exchanges, and my memory of them— memory being after all a function of the imagination—are and were like rhetorical tropes. Living ones, not literary ones, but tropes nonetheless. Perhaps the fact is that I "know" and "understand" Elizabeth Finch no better—if in a different way—than I "know" and "understand" the emperor Julian. So, realising this, it was time to stop.

I see her again, leaning towards me over the lunch table, after I had preferred veal escalope to pasta. "How is that?" she asks eagerly. "Disappointing?" As if she were asking about everything else as well—life, God, the weather, the government, death, love, sandwiches and the existence of unfinished masterpieces.

How about this: she plans to write a book about the emperor and his historical consequences, but can't make it work. Either because she doesn't have the skill. Or because the historical and theological complications defeat her. Or because Julian turns out not to be the man she first thought him. Or because her initial, grand audacity was not rewarded: "Thou hast conquered, O pale Galilean" did not lead by a traceable path to the emotional *froideur* and papal authoritarianism of Christian Europe—to both joyless, guilt-ridden Protestantism and to corrupt, guilt-ridden Catholicism. Or if it did so lead, she was not to be the path-finder.

And so she destroyed what she had written (before or after her "martyrdom"?) and bequeathed her preparatory notes and thoughts to another—me. Knowing, or not knowing, that she had passed them on to one notorious for his unfinished projects. Either way, she would have appreciated the irony.

Though she herself rarely left anything to chance, I think that, in a funny kind of way, she was doing just that by handing me the charge of her literary leavings. "In a funny kind of way"—well, she had a fine, ironic wit to her, we shouldn't forget that. It was chance whether or not I would have the energy or interest to follow a trail she had half-obliterated. Chance, too, whether I might attempt in some way to reconstruct her "book." Let alone—which she would not have foreseen—whether I would attempt to reconstruct her life.

So that is what I decided to do as well: let chance, let fortune have its way. I shall leave what I have written in a drawer, perhaps with EF's notebooks nearby. Occasionally, I imagine one of my children finding it after my death. "Oh look, Dad's written a book! Anyone want to read it?" "Probably another of his unfinished projects." "Like us." Then they might talk about my failings as a father. They might just shove my typescript back in the desk and leave the house-clearer to throw it in a skip. No, I do them an injustice. One of the three might feel a little sentimental, a little curious about what Dad had been up to. Perhaps another might carry off the notebooks, wondering who Elizabeth Finch was, and whether we had been lovers; but maybe they would disappoint—too many conclusions, not enough narrative—and be thrown out. My "book," if it merits the word, might be returned to a different drawer in a different desk, its next fate up to someone perhaps not yet born.

This would be just. Some things are up to us, and some things are not up to us. This thing is not now up to me, and so will not hinder me from attaining freedom and happiness.

And any ironic laughter you hear will be mine.

ACKNOWLEDGEMENTS

I would like to thank my brother Jonathan Barnes for saving me from much error; also Matthew Bell, Peter Bien, Vanessa Guignery, Christi Klinkert, Hermione Lee, Peter Millican, Sumaya Partner, Robert Priest, Stefan Rebenich, Ritchie Robertson and George Syrimis.

The lyric quoted on page 95 is from "Well, Did You Evah?," words and music by Cole Porter ©1956 Chappell & Co. Inc. (ASCAP), all rights administered by Warner Chappell North America Ltd.

A NOTE ABOUT THE AUTHOR

Julian Barnes is the author of twenty-four previous books, for which he has received the Man Booker Prize, the Somerset Maugham Award, the E. M. Forster Award from the American Academy of Arts and Letters, and the Prix Médicis and Prix Femina. In 2017 he was awarded the Légion d'honneur. His work has been translated into more than forty languages. He lives in London.

A NOTE ON THE TYPE

This book was set in a version of the well-known
Monotype face Bembo. This letter was cut for the
celebrated Venetian printer Aldus Manutius by Fran-
cesco Griffo, and first used in Pietro Cardinal Bembo's
De Aetna of 1495.

The companion italic is an adaptation of the chan-
cery script type designed by the calligrapher and printer
Lodovico degli Arrighi.

Printed and bound by Berryville Graphics,
Berryville, Virginia